— Jack London's —
White Fang

Adapted by
Joeming Dunn

Illustrated by
Cynthia Martin

magic
wagon

visit us at
www.abdopublishing.com

Published by Magic Wagon, a division of the ABDO Publishing Group, 8000 West 78th Street, Edina, Minnesota 55439. Copyright © 2008 by Abdo Consulting Group, Inc. International copyrights reserved in all countries. All rights reserved. No part of this book may be reproduced in any form without written permission from the publisher. Graphic Planet™ is a trademark and logo of Magic Wagon.

Printed in the United States of America, North Mankato, Minnesota.

Original novel by Jack London
Adapted by Joeming Dunn
Illustrated by Cynthia Martin
Colored by Rod Espinosa and Robert Acosta
Lettered by Joeming Dunn
Edited by Stephanie Hedlund
Interior layout and design by Antarctic Press
Cover art by Ben Dunn
Cover design by Neil Klinepier

Library of Congress Cataloging-in-Publication Data

Dunn, Joeming W.
   White Fang / Jack London ; adapted by Joeming Dunn ; illustrated by Cynthia Martin.
   p. cm. -- (Graphic classics)
   Includes bibliographical references.
   ISBN 978-1-60270-055-0
   1. Graphic novels. I. Martin, Cynthia, 1961- . II. London, Jack, 1876-1916. White Fang. III. Title.

PN6727.D89W55 2008
741.5'973--dc22

                                     2007006446

012008
022010

TABLE of CONTENTS

Chapter 1 The Wolf Pack

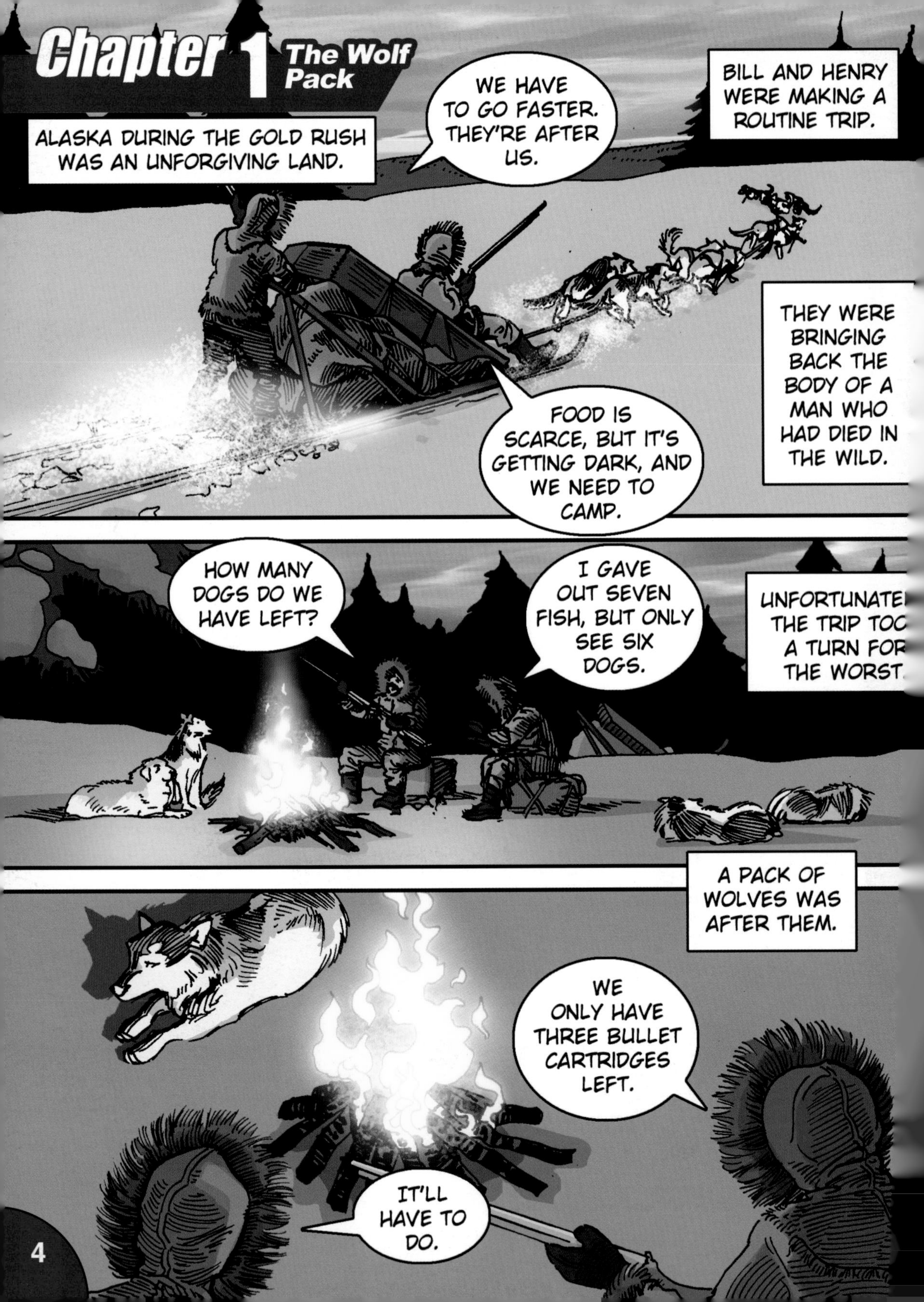
ALASKA DURING THE GOLD RUSH WAS AN UNFORGIVING LAND.
WE HAVE TO GO FASTER. THEY'RE AFTER US.
BILL AND HENRY WERE MAKING A ROUTINE TRIP.
THEY WERE BRINGING BACK THE BODY OF A MAN WHO HAD DIED IN THE WILD.
FOOD IS SCARCE, BUT IT'S GETTING DARK, AND WE NEED TO CAMP.
HOW MANY DOGS DO WE HAVE LEFT?
I GAVE OUT SEVEN FISH, BUT ONLY SEE SIX DOGS.
UNFORTUNATE THE TRIP TOO A TURN FOR THE WORST
A PACK OF WOLVES WAS AFTER THEM.
WE ONLY HAVE THREE BULLET CARTRIDGES LEFT.
IT'LL HAVE TO DO.

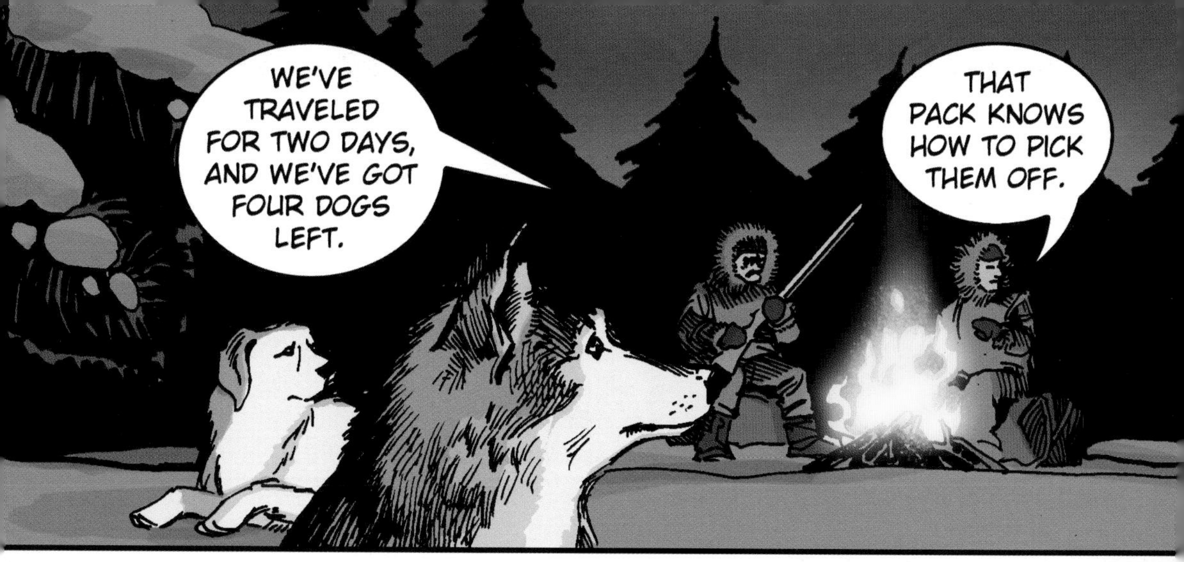
WE'VE TRAVELED FOR TWO DAYS, AND WE'VE GOT FOUR DOGS LEFT.
THAT PACK KNOWS HOW TO PICK THEM OFF.

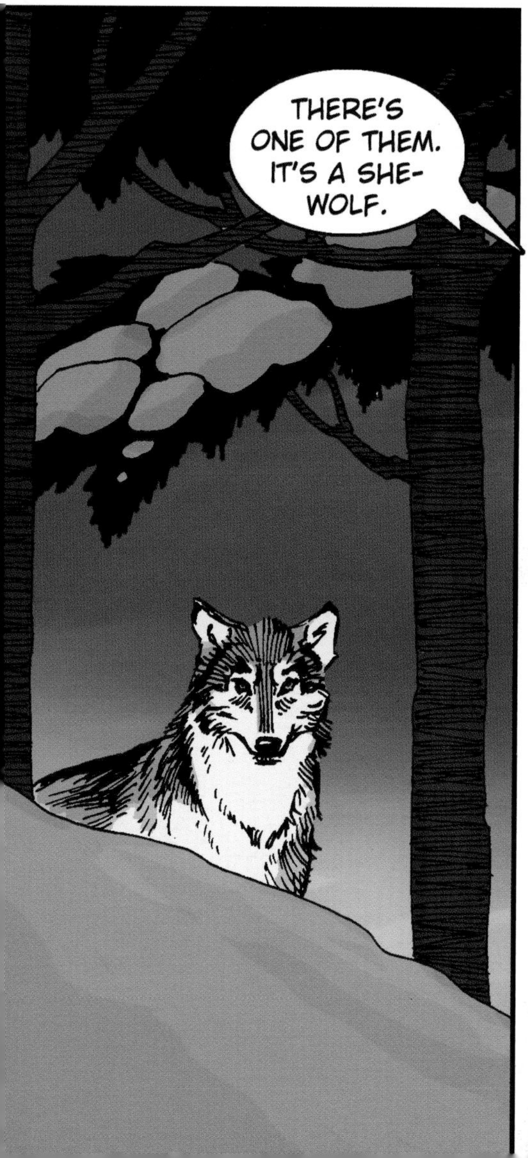
THERE'S ONE OF THEM. IT'S A SHE-WOLF.

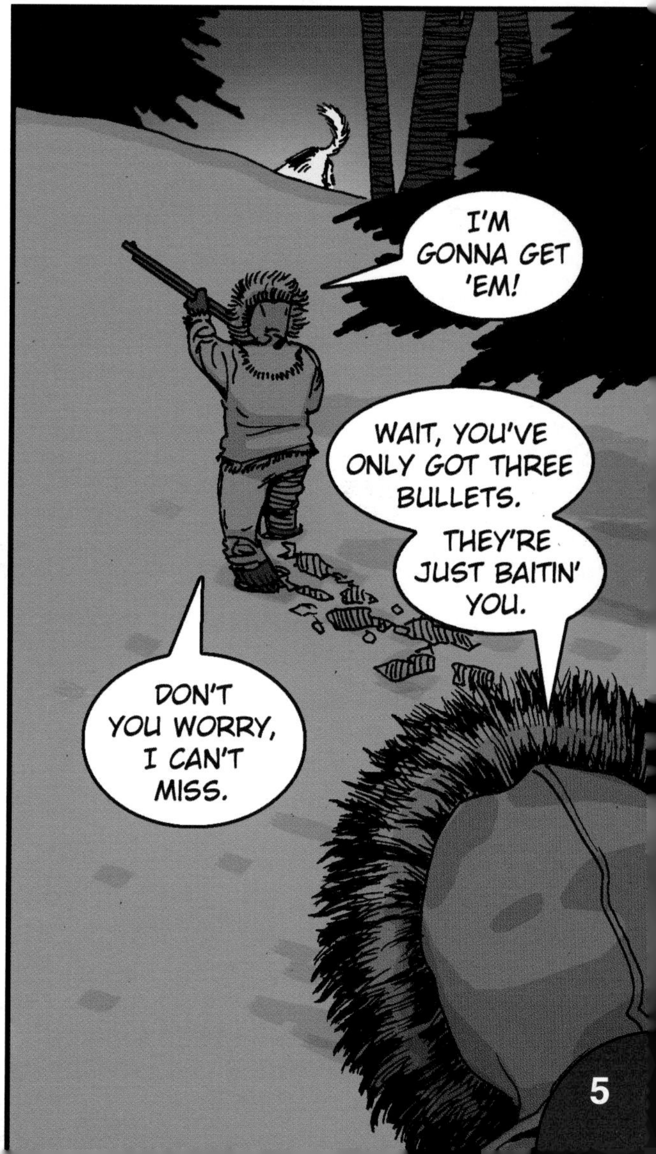
I'M GONNA GET 'EM!
WAIT, YOU'VE ONLY GOT THREE BULLETS.
THEY'RE JUST BAITIN' YOU.
DON'T YOU WORRY, I CAN'T MISS.

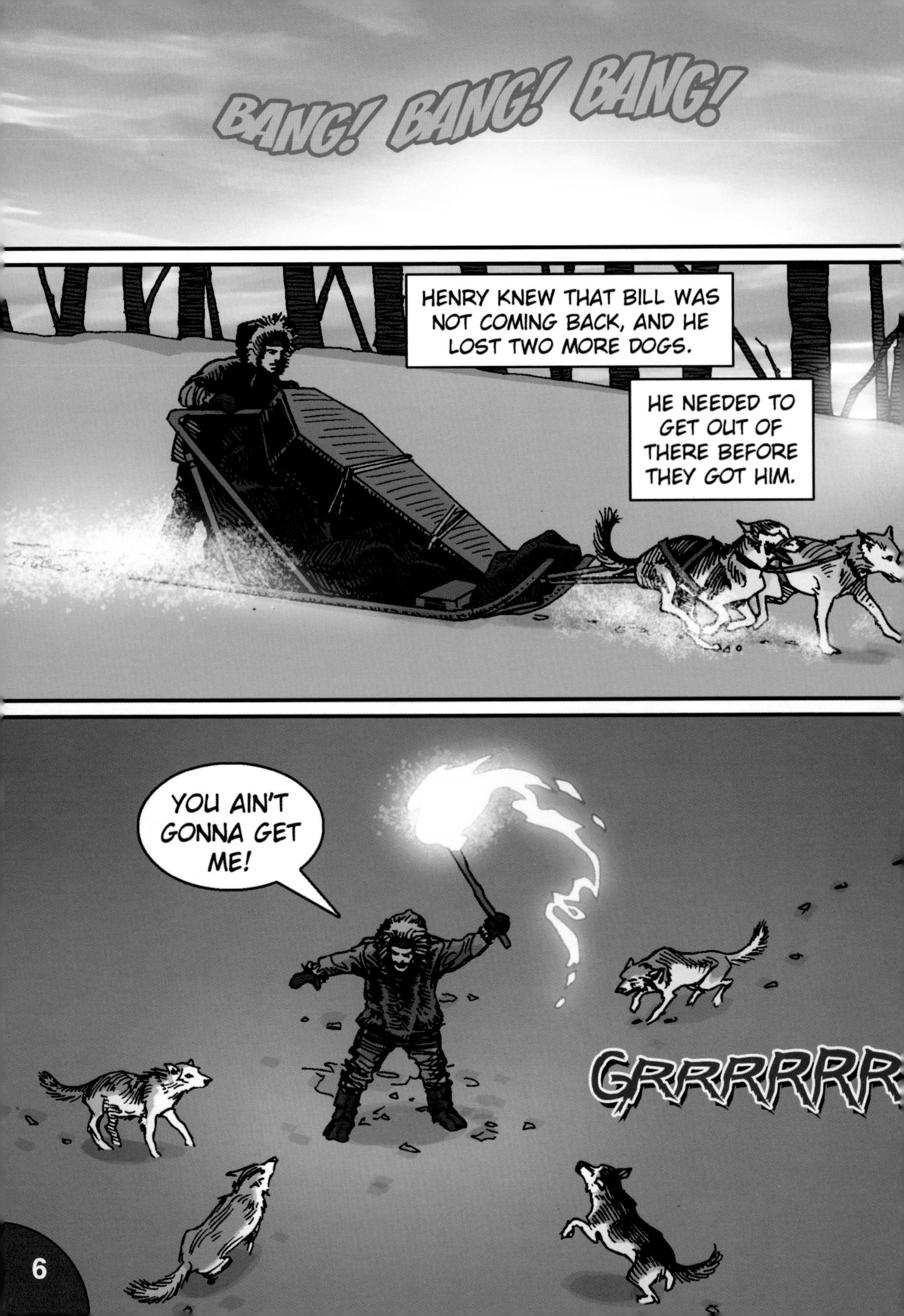
BANG! BANG! BANG!
HENRY KNEW THAT BILL WAS NOT COMING BACK, AND HE LOST TWO MORE DOGS.
HE NEEDED TO GET OUT OF THERE BEFORE THEY GOT HIM.
YOU AIN'T GONNA GET ME!
GRRRRRR

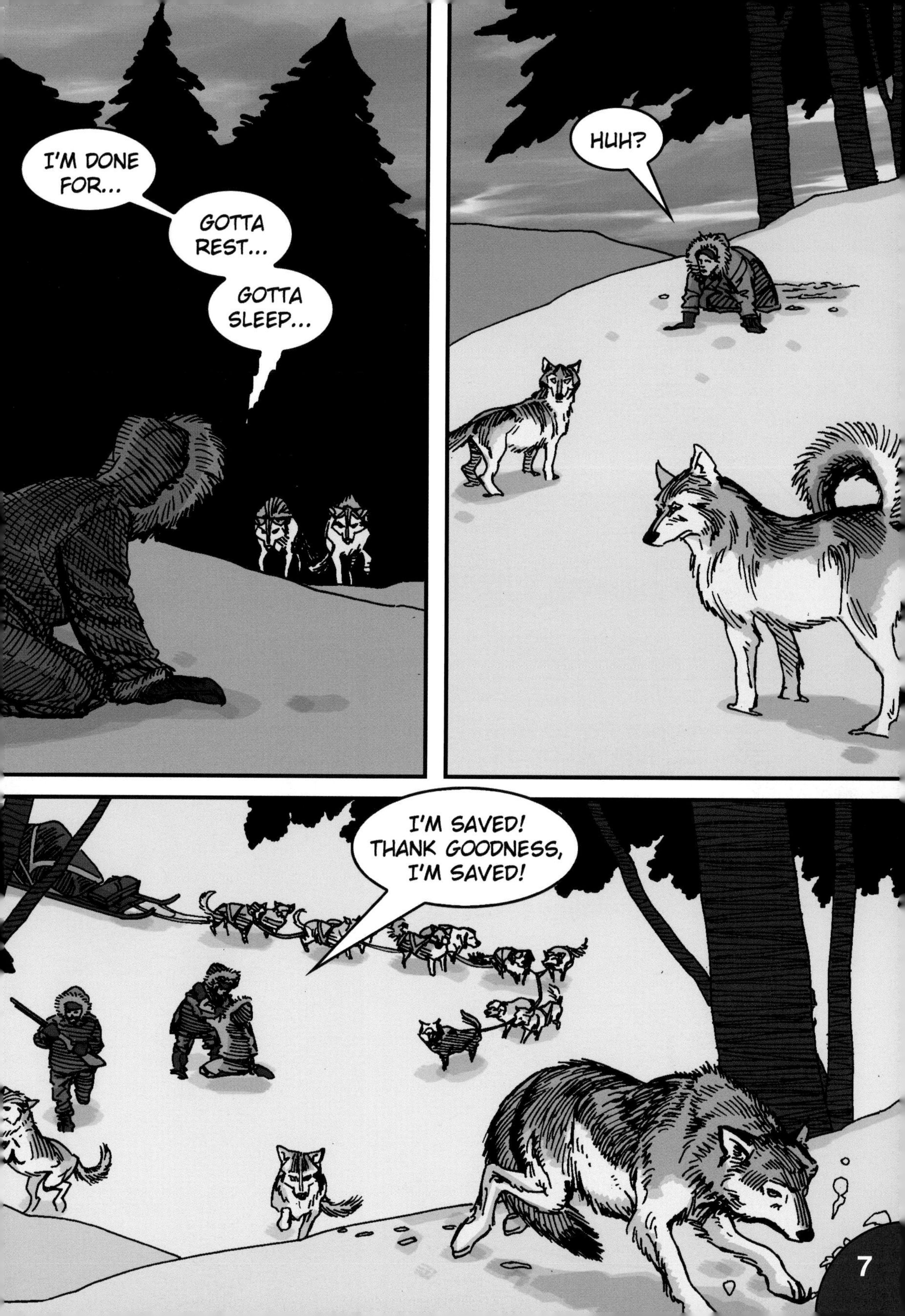
I'M DONE FOR...
GOTTA REST...
GOTTA SLEEP...
HUH?
I'M SAVED! THANK GOODNESS, I'M SAVED!

Chapter 2 The Birth of White Fang

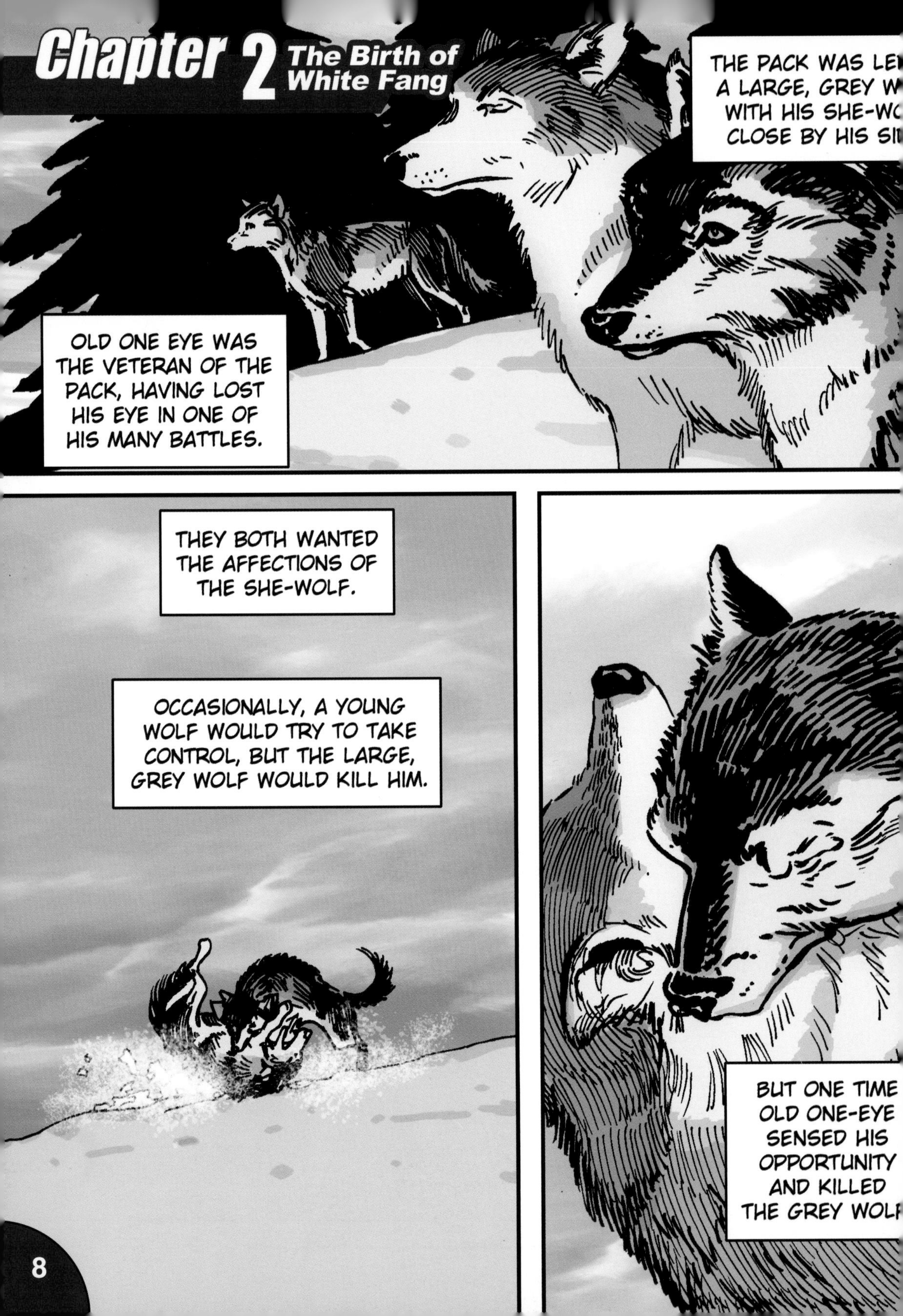
THE PACK WAS LE
A LARGE, GREY W
WITH HIS SHE-WO
CLOSE BY HIS SI
OLD ONE EYE WAS THE VETERAN OF THE PACK, HAVING LOST HIS EYE IN ONE OF HIS MANY BATTLES.
THEY BOTH WANTED THE AFFECTIONS OF THE SHE-WOLF.
OCCASIONALLY, A YOUNG WOLF WOULD TRY TO TAKE CONTROL, BUT THE LARGE, GREY WOLF WOULD KILL HIM.
BUT ONE TIME OLD ONE-EYE SENSED HIS OPPORTUNITY AND KILLED THE GREY WOL

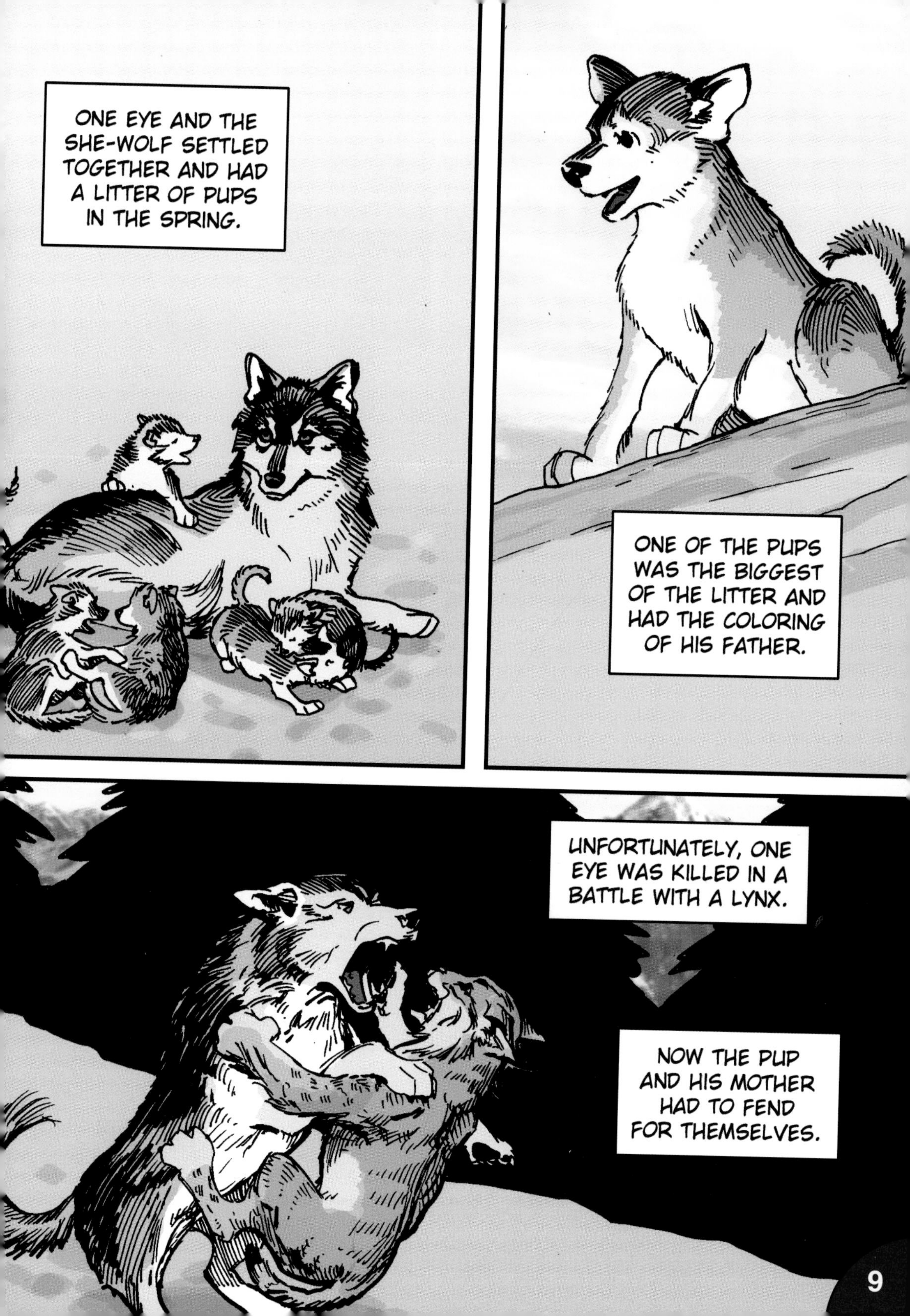
ONE EYE AND THE SHE-WOLF SETTLED TOGETHER AND HAD A LITTER OF PUPS IN THE SPRING.
ONE OF THE PUPS WAS THE BIGGEST OF THE LITTER AND HAD THE COLORING OF HIS FATHER.
UNFORTUNATELY, ONE EYE WAS KILLED IN A BATTLE WITH A LYNX.
NOW THE PUP AND HIS MOTHER HAD TO FEND FOR THEMSELVES.

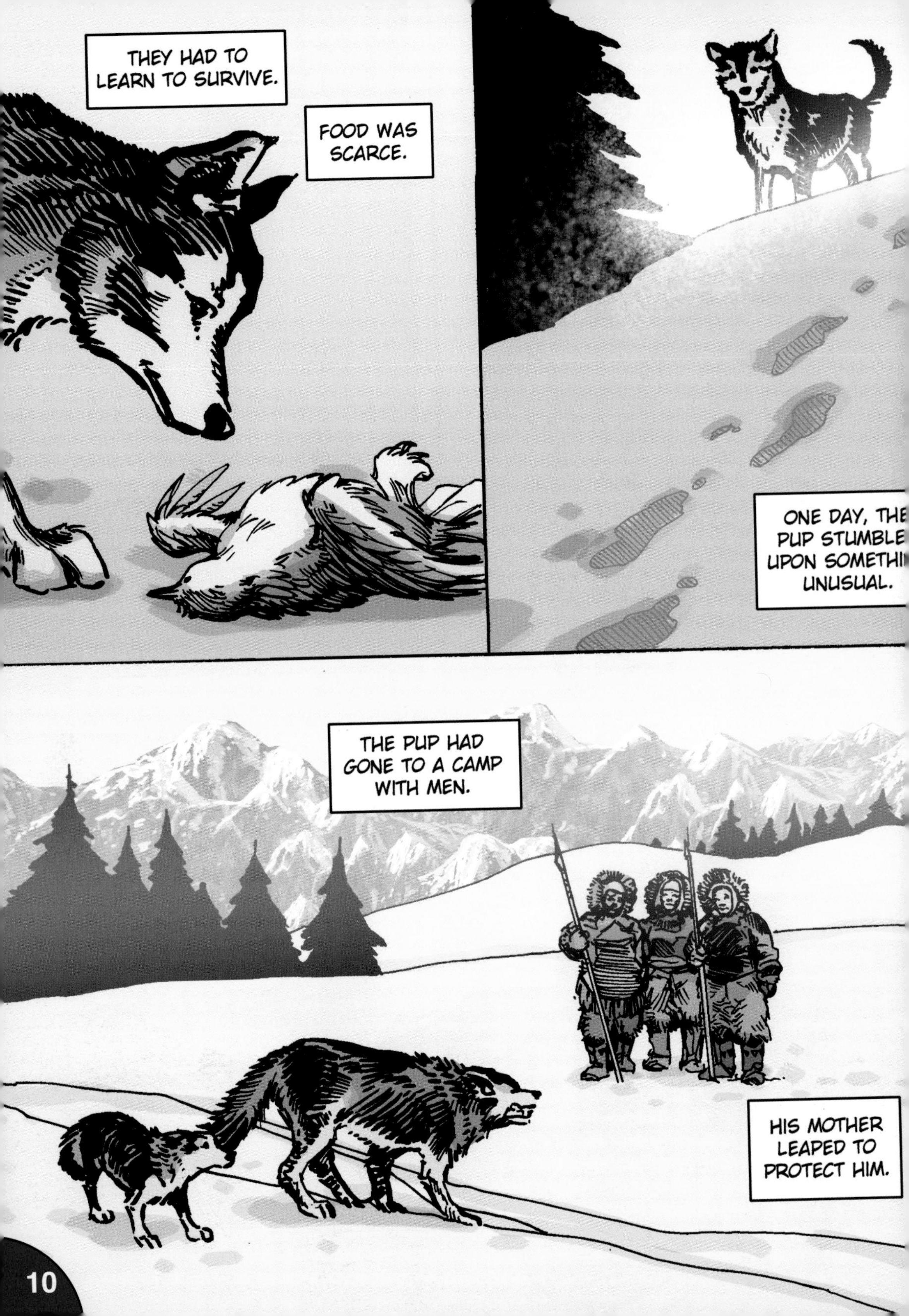
THEY HAD TO LEARN TO SURVIVE.
FOOD WAS SCARCE.
ONE DAY, THE PUP STUMBLE UPON SOMETHI UNUSUAL.
THE PUP HAD GONE TO A CAMP WITH MEN.
HIS MOTHER LEAPED TO PROTECT HIM.

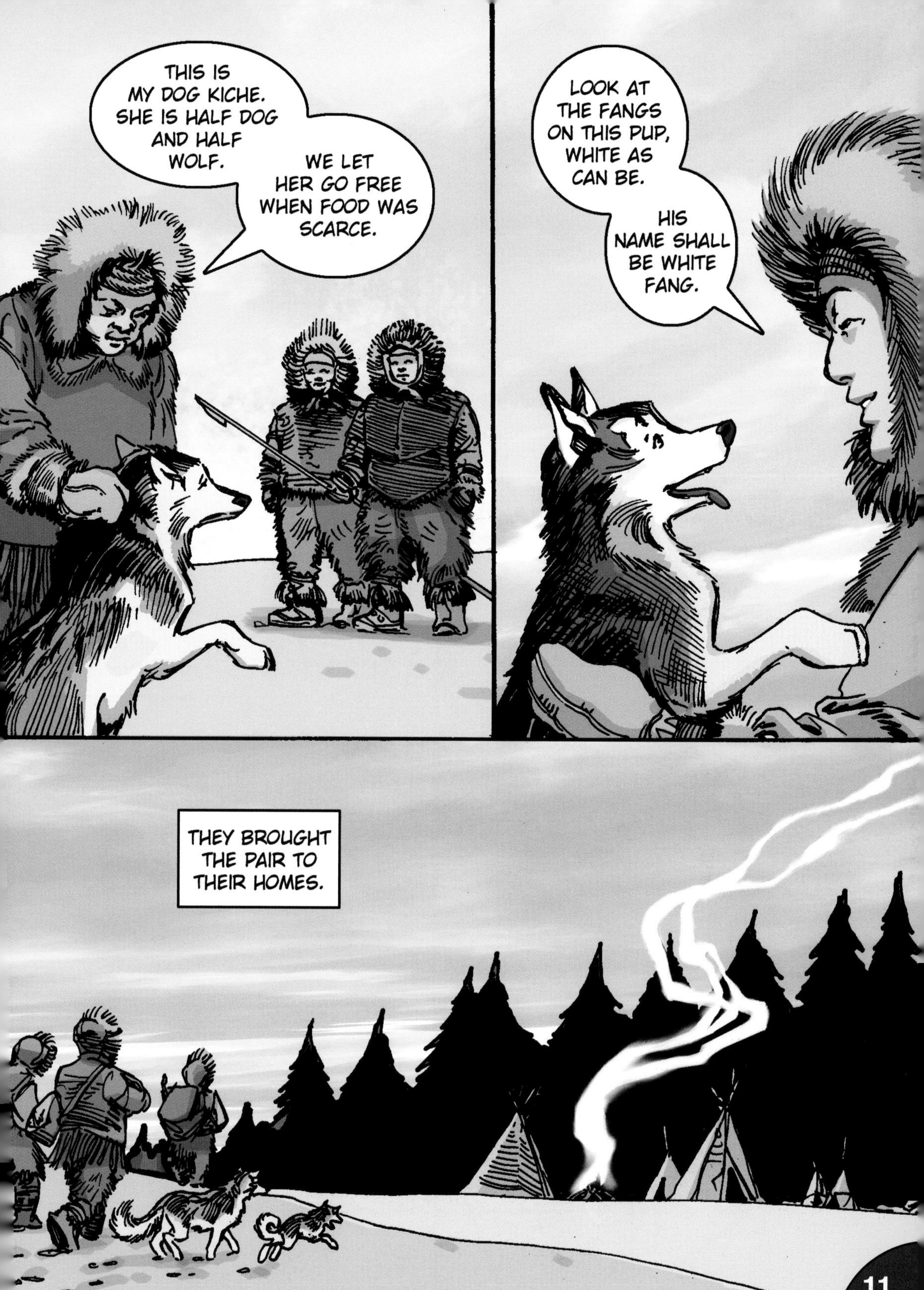
THIS IS MY DOG KICHE. SHE IS HALF DOG AND HALF WOLF.
WE LET HER GO FREE WHEN FOOD WAS SCARCE.
LOOK AT THE FANGS ON THIS PUP, WHITE AS CAN BE.
HIS NAME SHALL BE WHITE FANG.
THEY BROUGHT THE PAIR TO THEIR HOMES.

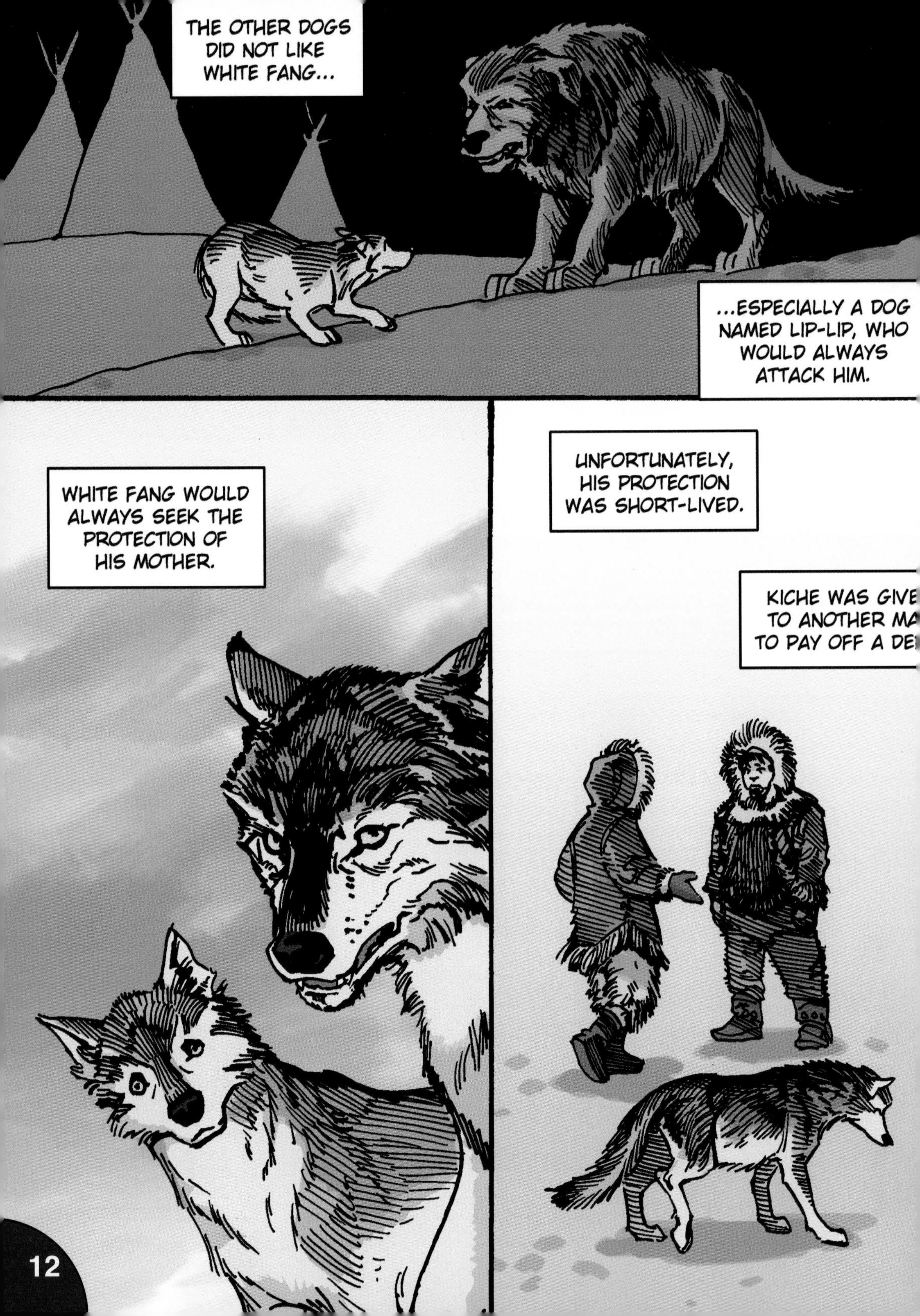
THE OTHER DOGS DID NOT LIKE WHITE FANG...
...ESPECIALLY A DOG NAMED LIP-LIP, WHO WOULD ALWAYS ATTACK HIM.
WHITE FANG WOULD ALWAYS SEEK THE PROTECTION OF HIS MOTHER.
UNFORTUNATELY, HIS PROTECTION WAS SHORT-LIVED.
KICHE WAS GIVE
TO ANOTHER MA
TO PAY OFF A DE

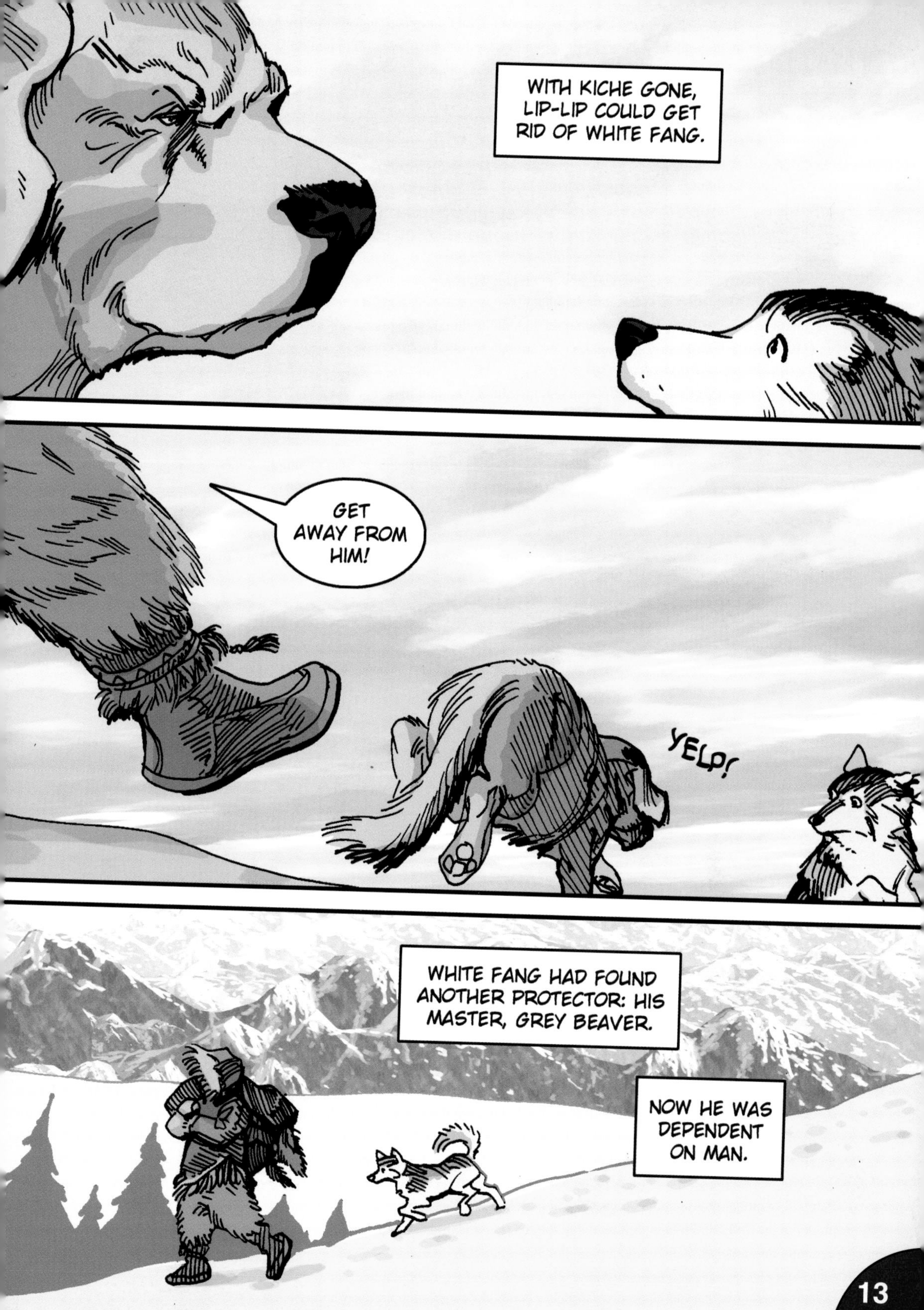
WITH KICHE GONE, LIP-LIP COULD GET RID OF WHITE FANG.
GET AWAY FROM HIM!
YELP!
WHITE FANG HAD FOUND ANOTHER PROTECTOR: HIS MASTER, GREY BEAVER.
NOW HE WAS DEPENDENT ON MAN.

Chapter 3 Surviving Alone

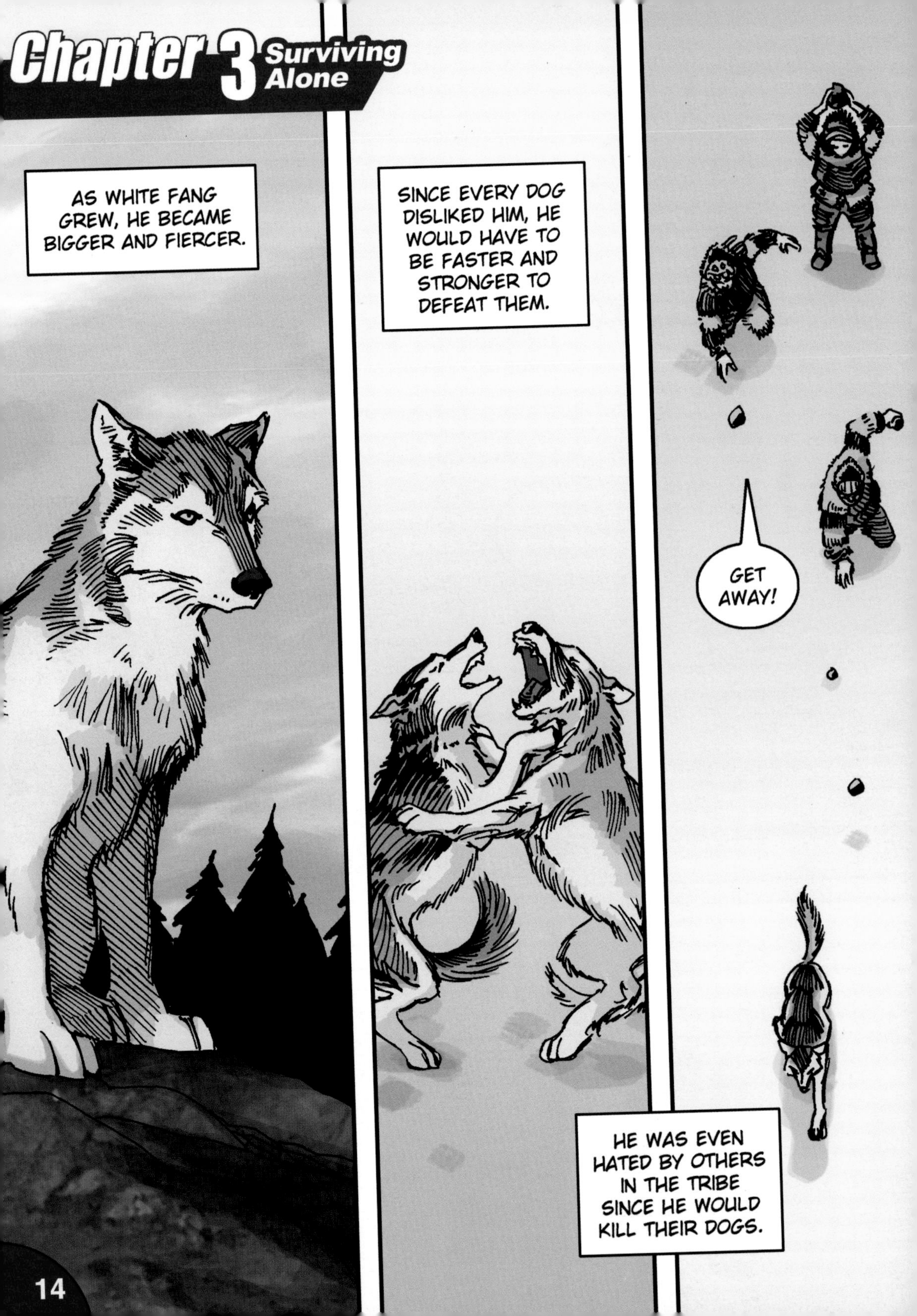

AS WHITE FANG GREW, HE BECAME BIGGER AND FIERCER.
SINCE EVERY DOG DISLIKED HIM, HE WOULD HAVE TO BE FASTER AND STRONGER TO DEFEAT THEM.
GET AWAY!
HE WAS EVEN HATED BY OTHERS IN THE TRIBE SINCE HE WOULD KILL THEIR DOGS.

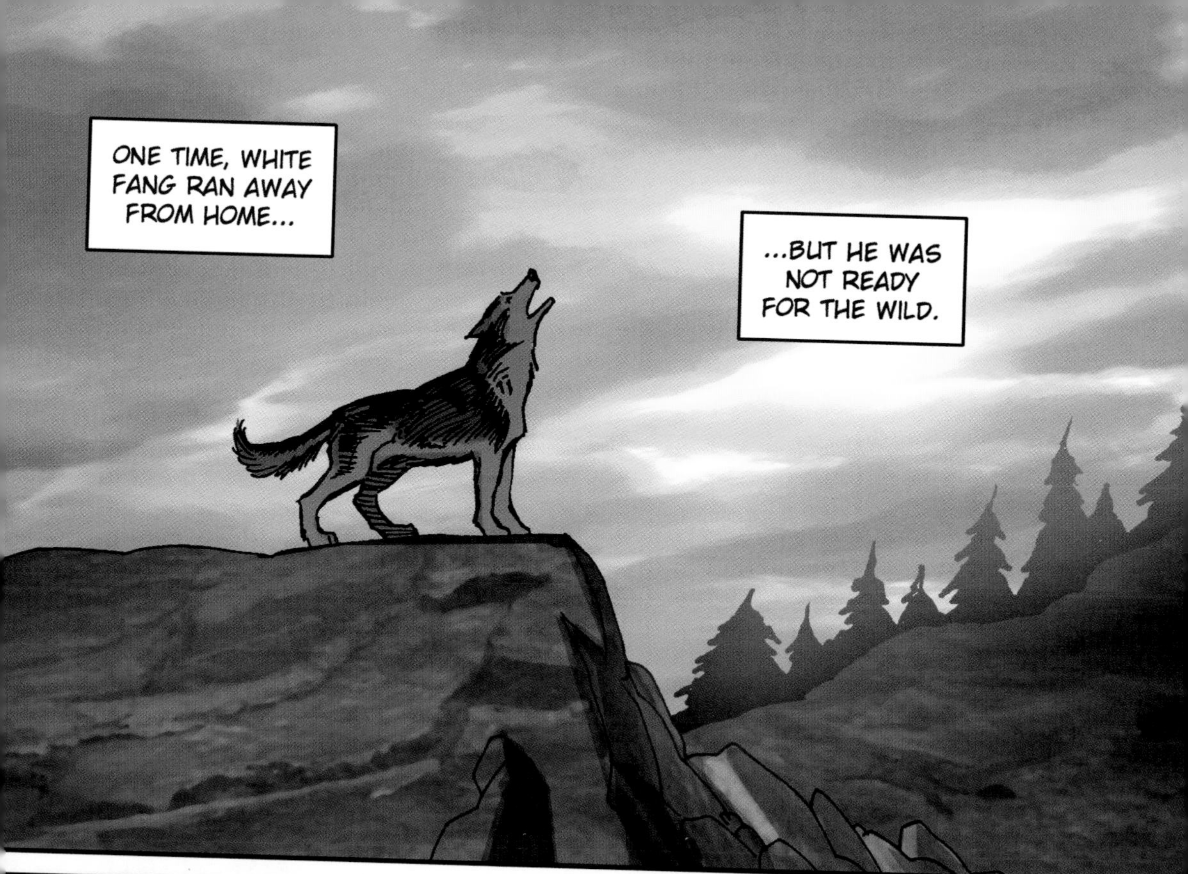
ONE TIME, WHITE FANG RAN AWAY FROM HOME...
...BUT HE WAS NOT READY FOR THE WILD.

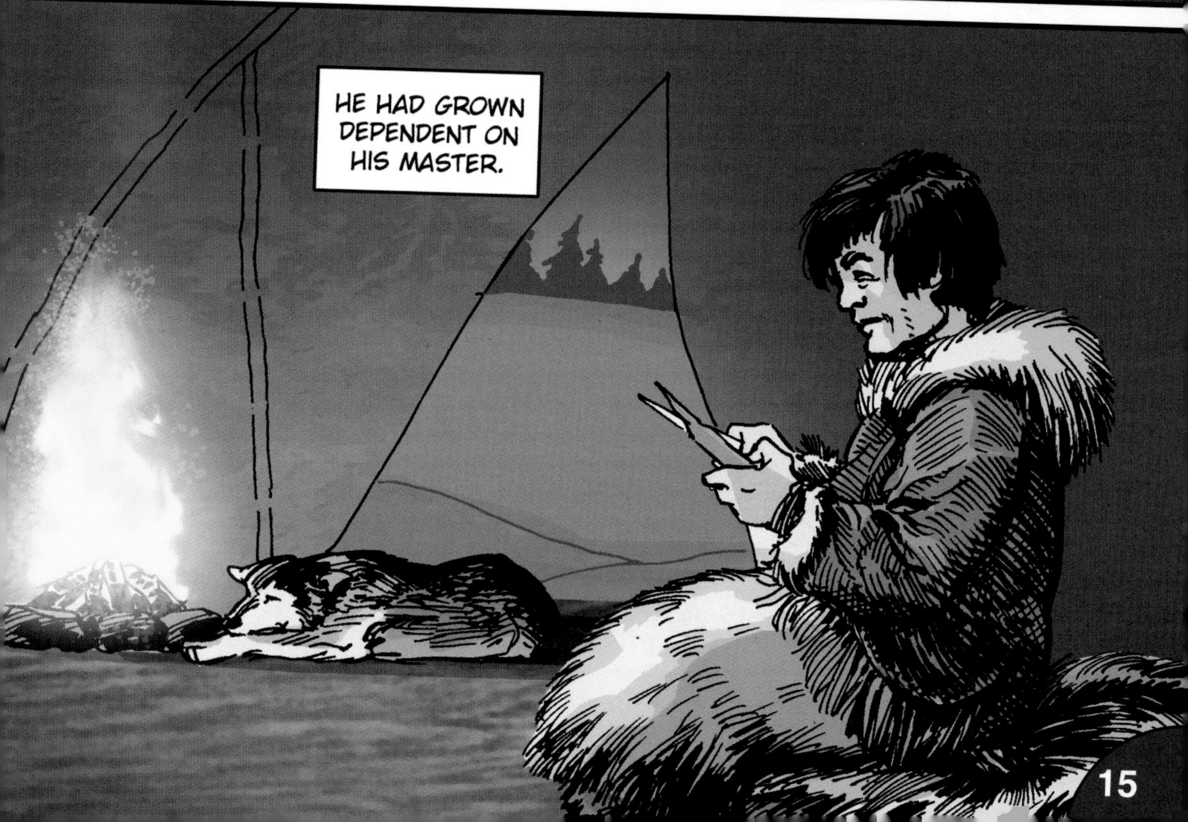
HE HAD GROWN DEPENDENT ON HIS MASTER.

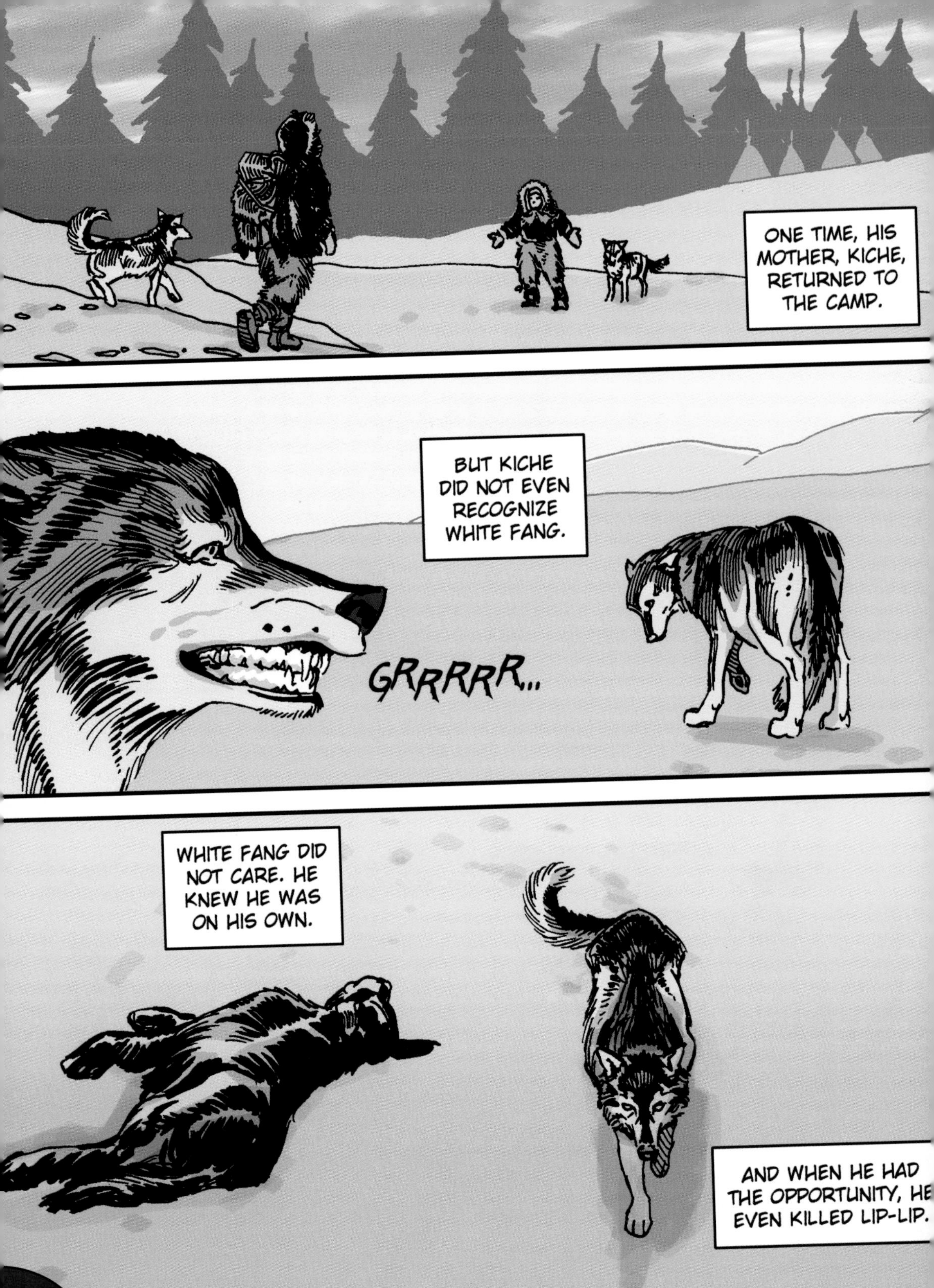
ONE TIME, HIS MOTHER, KICHE, RETURNED TO THE CAMP.
BUT KICHE DID NOT EVEN RECOGNIZE WHITE FANG.
GRRRRR...
WHITE FANG DID NOT CARE. HE KNEW HE WAS ON HIS OWN.
AND WHEN HE HAD THE OPPORTUNITY, HE EVEN KILLED LIP-LIP.

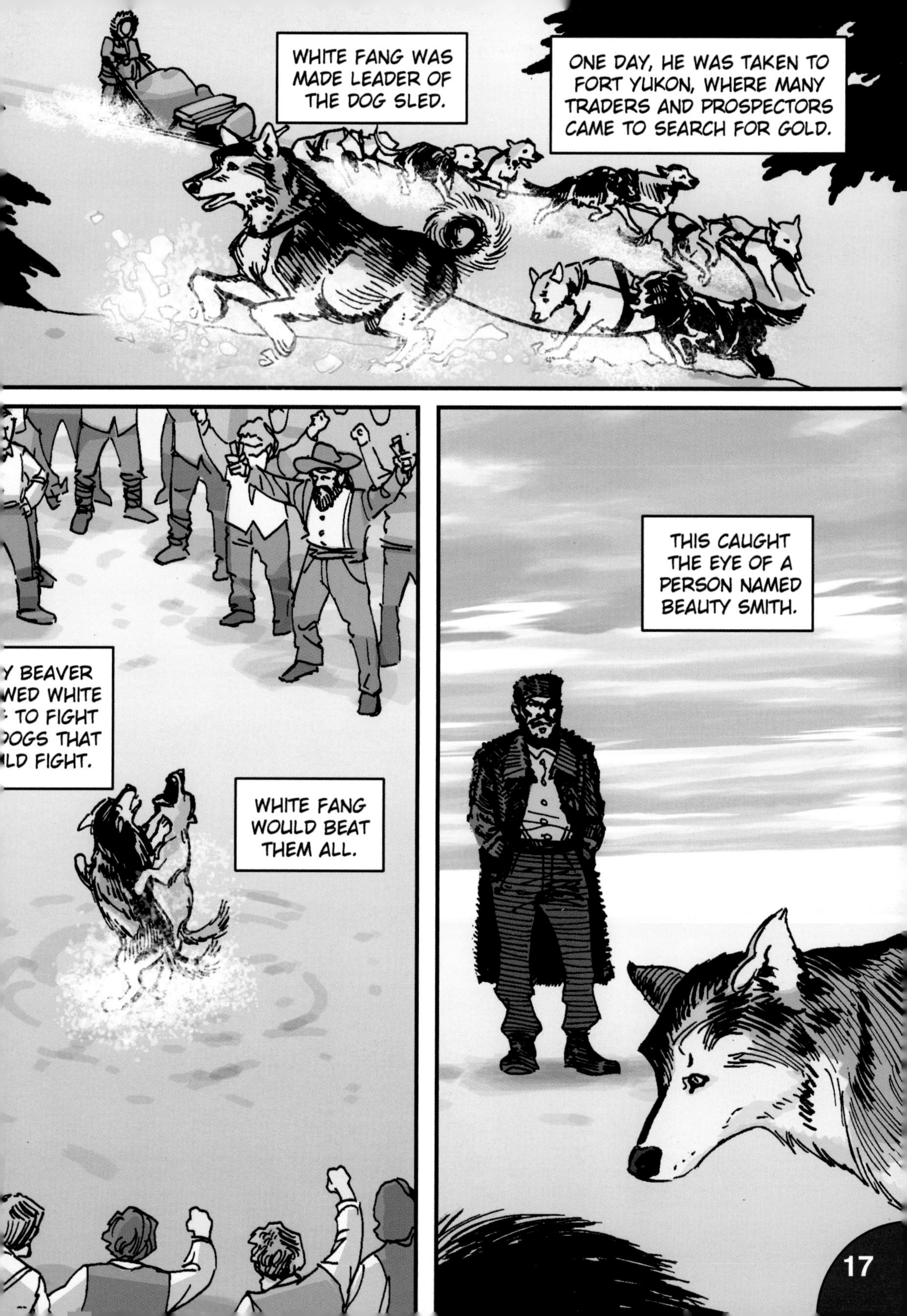
WHITE FANG WAS MADE LEADER OF THE DOG SLED.
ONE DAY, HE WAS TAKEN TO FORT YUKON, WHERE MANY TRADERS AND PROSPECTORS CAME TO SEARCH FOR GOLD.
Y BEAVER WED WHITE TO FIGHT OGS THAT LD FIGHT.
WHITE FANG WOULD BEAT THEM ALL.
THIS CAUGHT THE EYE OF A PERSON NAMED BEAUTY SMITH.

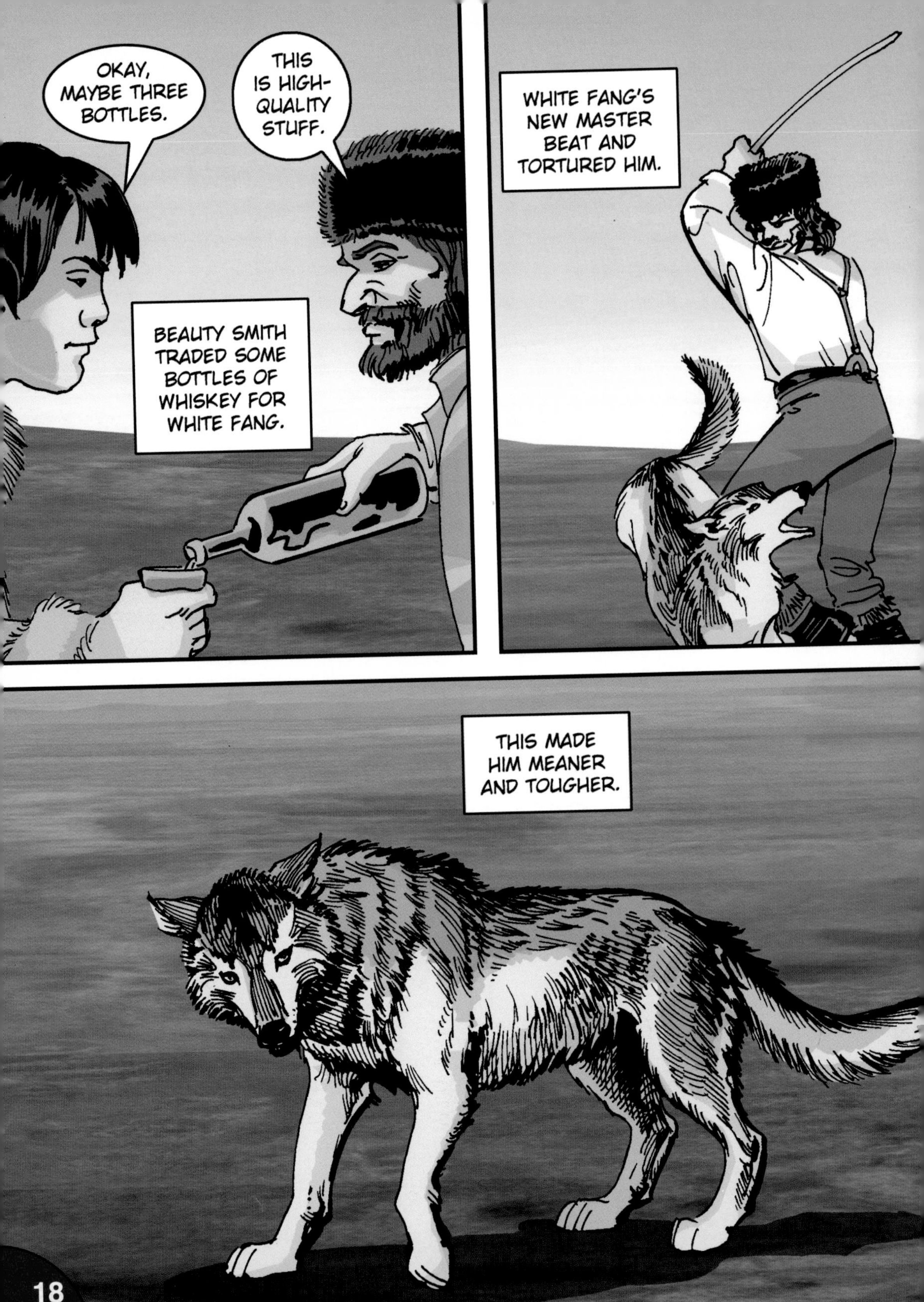
OKAY, MAYBE THREE BOTTLES.
THIS IS HIGH-QUALITY STUFF.
BEAUTY SMITH TRADED SOME BOTTLES OF WHISKEY FOR WHITE FANG.
WHITE FANG'S NEW MASTER BEAT AND TORTURED HIM.
THIS MADE HIM MEANER AND TOUGHER.

apter 4 The Dogfighting Ring

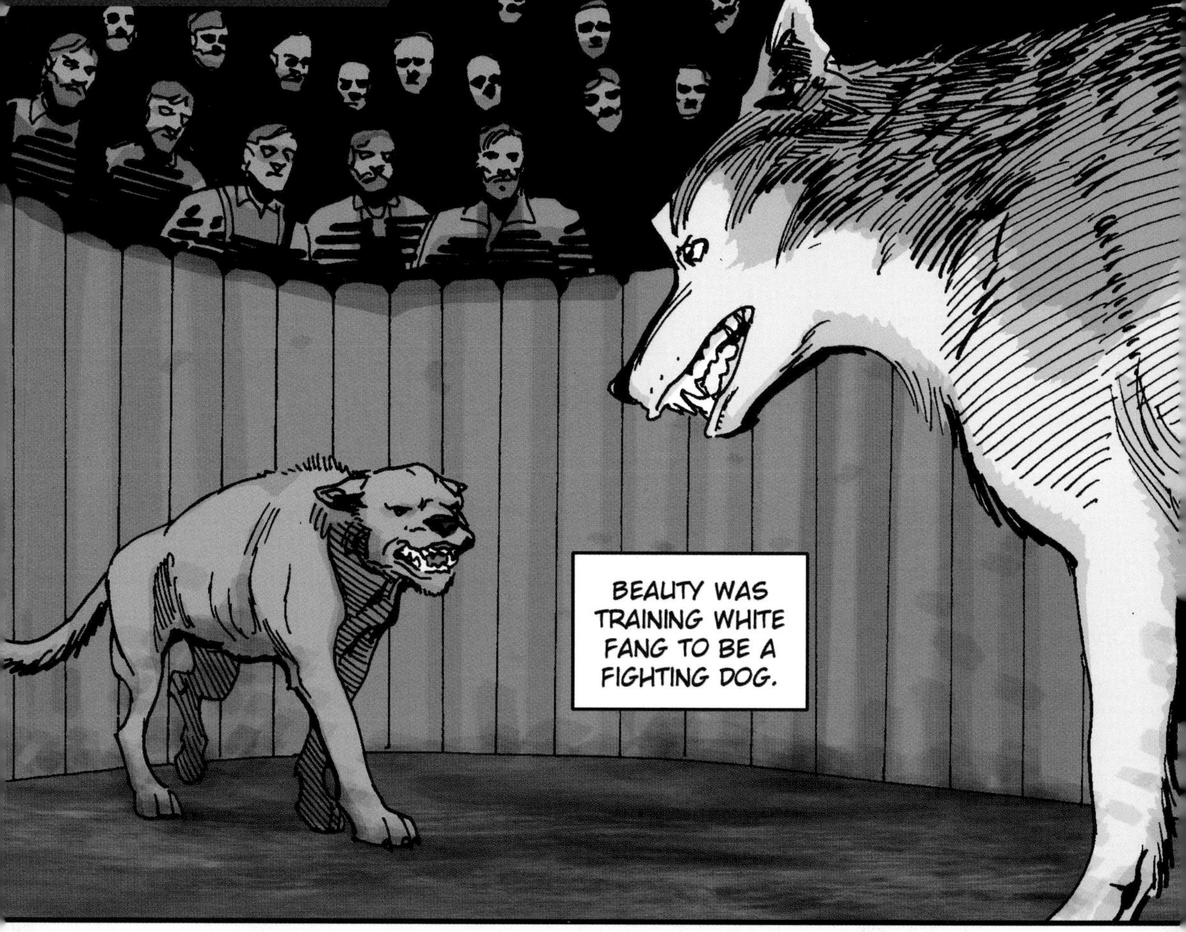
BEAUTY WAS TRAINING WHITE FANG TO BE A FIGHTING DOG.

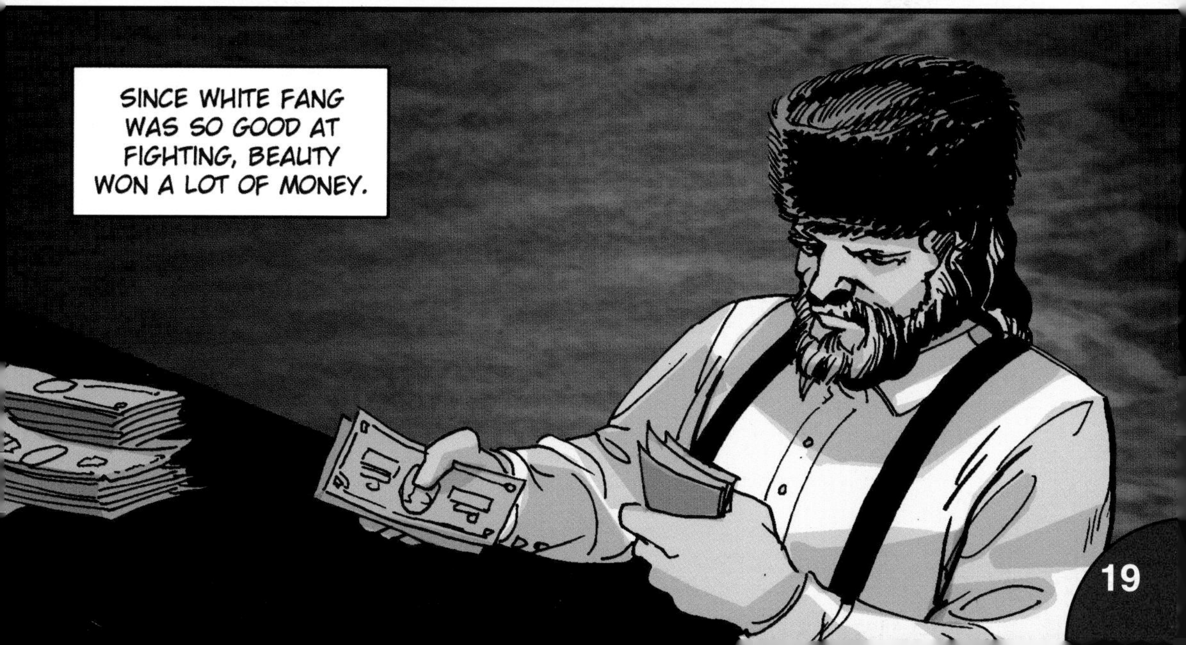
SINCE WHITE FANG WAS SO GOOD AT FIGHTING, BEAUTY WON A LOT OF MONEY.

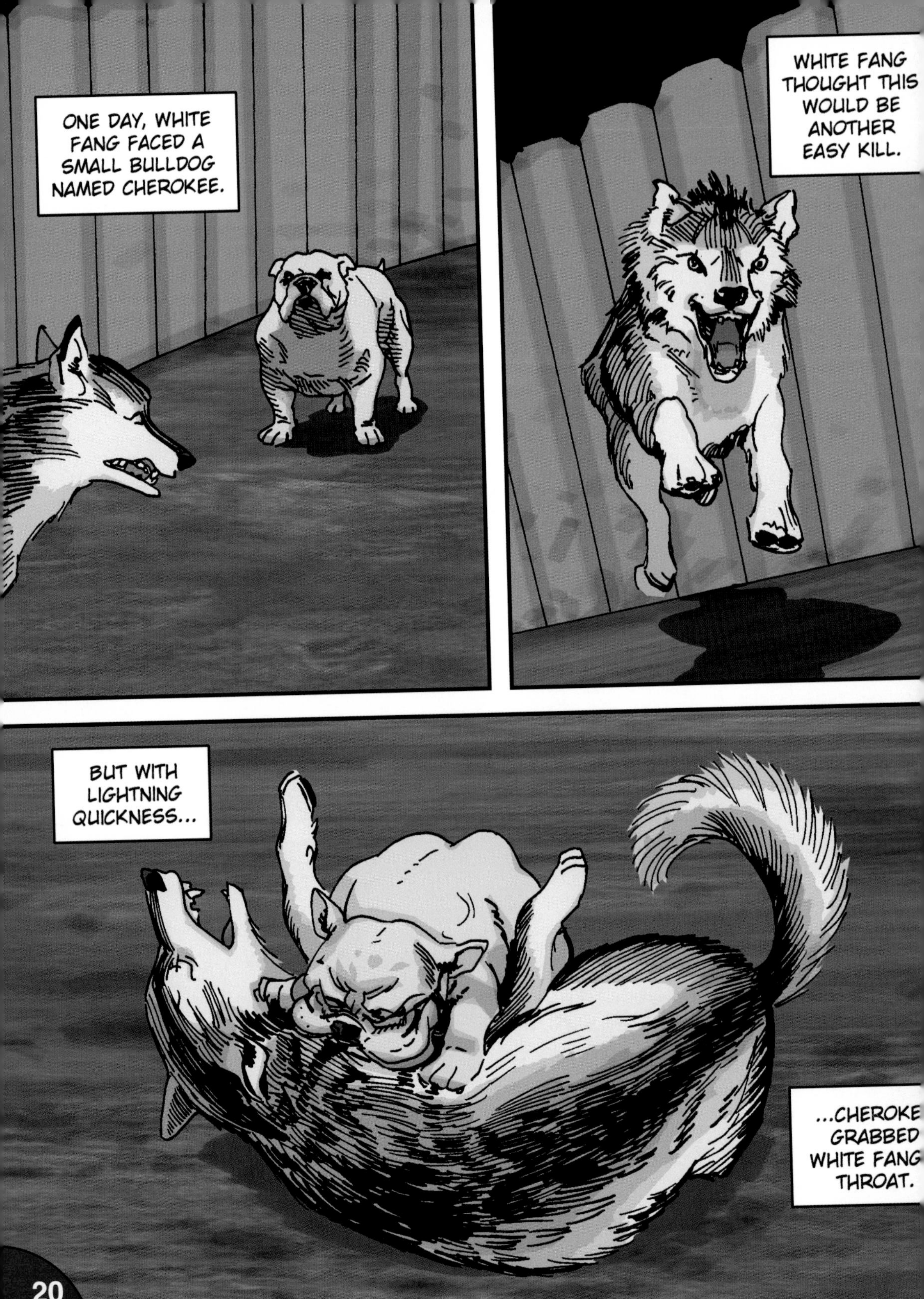
ONE DAY, WHITE FANG FACED A SMALL BULLDOG NAMED CHEROKEE.
WHITE FANG THOUGHT THIS WOULD BE ANOTHER EASY KILL.
BUT WITH LIGHTNING QUICKNESS...
...CHEROKE GRABBED WHITE FANG THROAT.

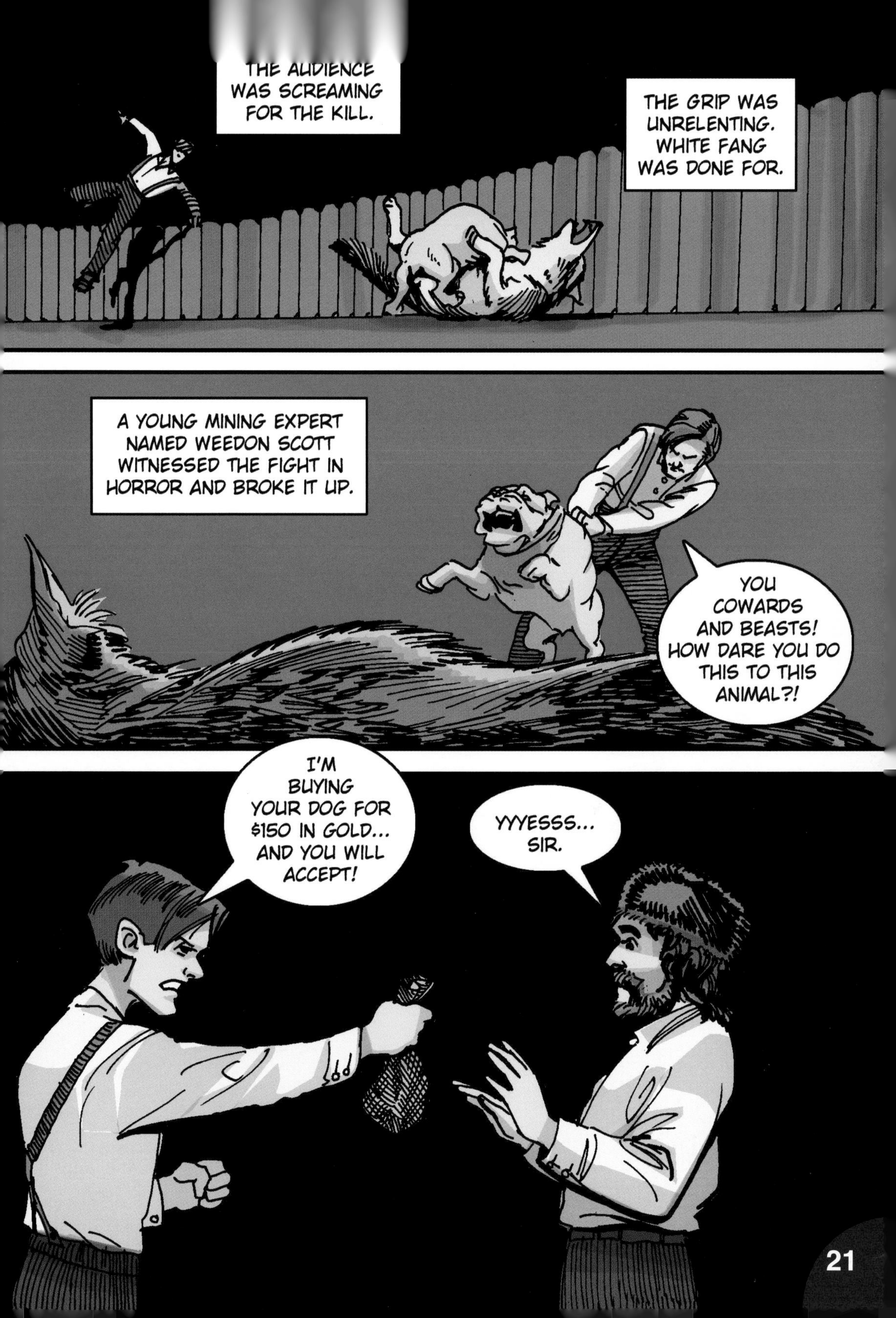
THE AUDIENCE WAS SCREAMING FOR THE KILL.
THE GRIP WAS UNRELENTING. WHITE FANG WAS DONE FOR.
A YOUNG MINING EXPERT NAMED WEEDON SCOTT WITNESSED THE FIGHT IN HORROR AND BROKE IT UP.
YOU COWARDS AND BEASTS! HOW DARE YOU DO THIS TO THIS ANIMAL?!
I'M BUYING YOUR DOG FOR $150 IN GOLD... AND YOU WILL ACCEPT!
YYYESSS... SIR.

Chapter 5 A New Owner

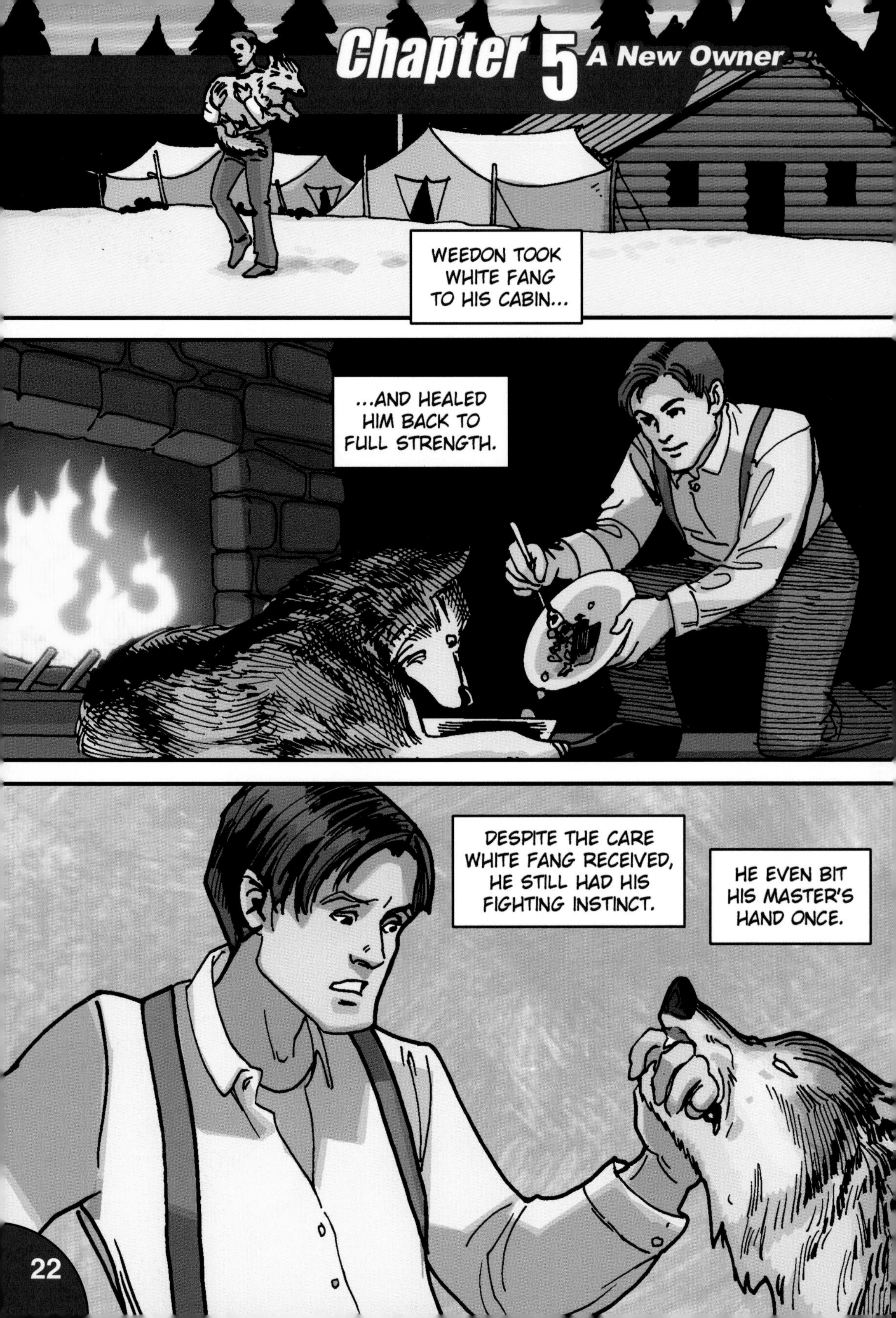
WEEDON TOOK WHITE FANG TO HIS CABIN...
...AND HEALED HIM BACK TO FULL STRENGTH.
DESPITE THE CARE WHITE FANG RECEIVED, HE STILL HAD HIS FIGHTING INSTINCT.
HE EVEN BIT HIS MASTER'S HAND ONCE.

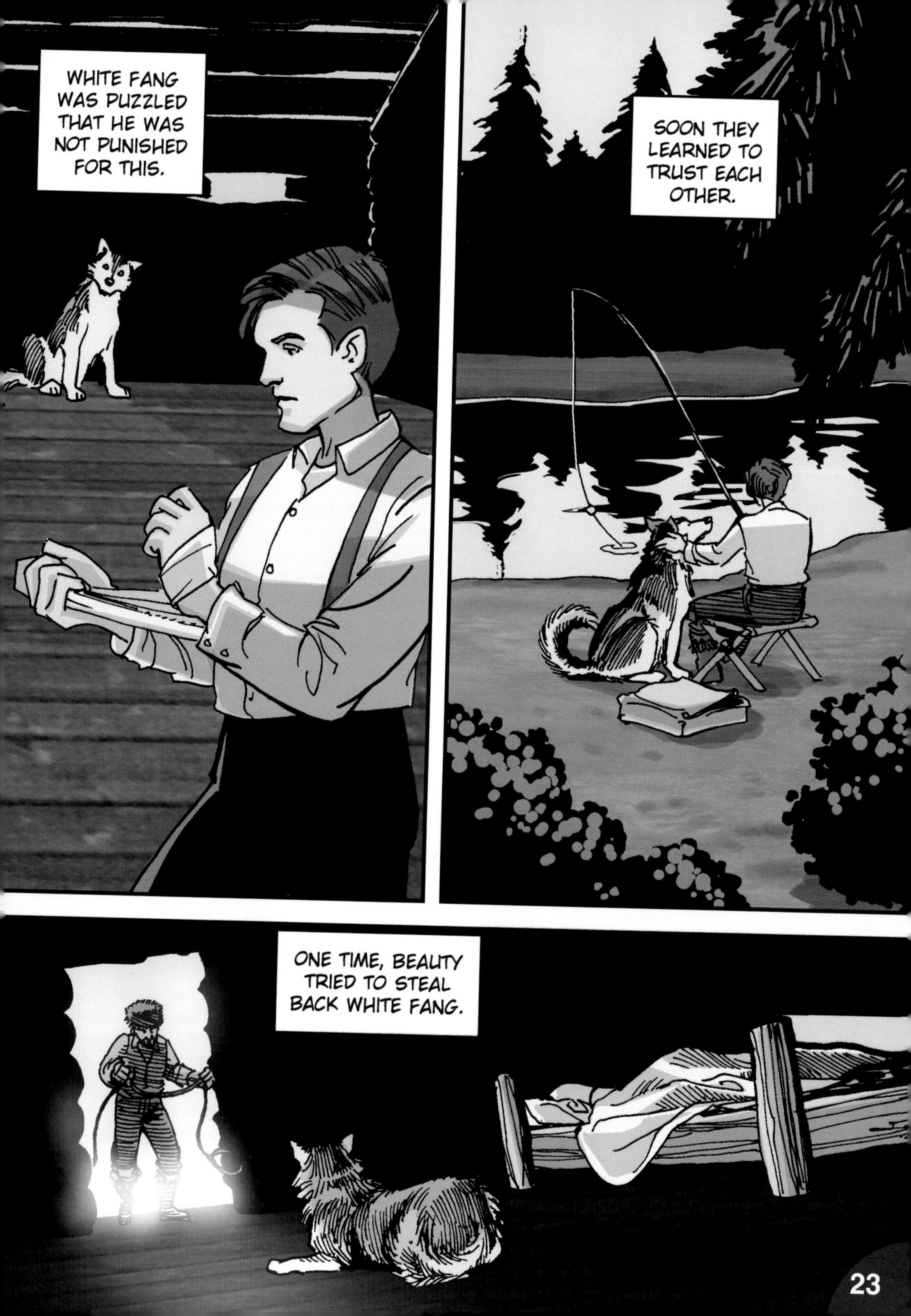
WHITE FANG WAS PUZZLED THAT HE WAS NOT PUNISHED FOR THIS.
SOON THEY LEARNED TO TRUST EACH OTHER.
ONE TIME, BEAUTY TRIED TO STEAL BACK WHITE FANG.

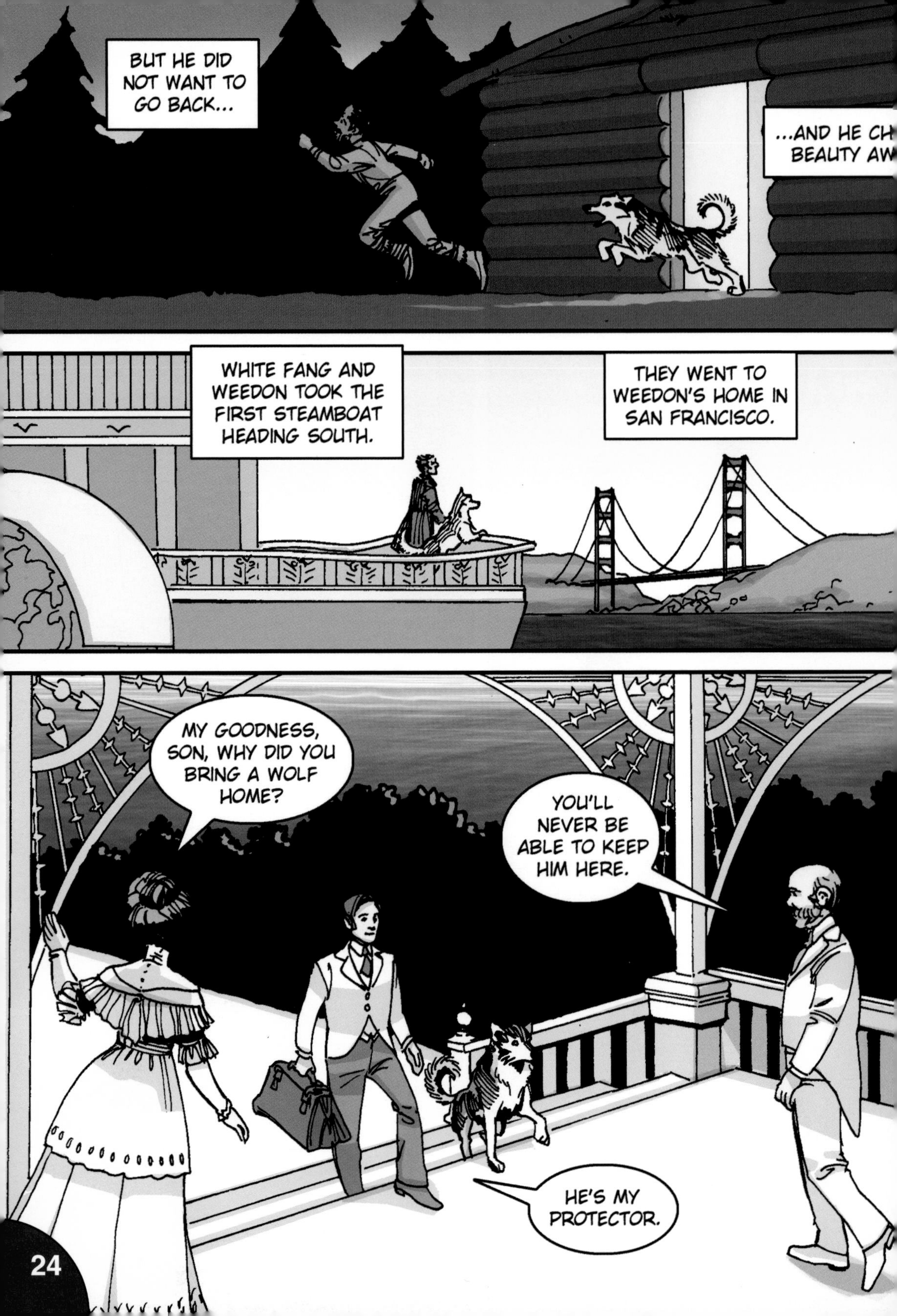
BUT HE DID NOT WANT TO GO BACK...
...AND HE CH BEAUTY AW
WHITE FANG AND WEEDON TOOK THE FIRST STEAMBOAT HEADING SOUTH.
THEY WENT TO WEEDON'S HOME IN SAN FRANCISCO.
MY GOODNESS, SON, WHY DID YOU BRING A WOLF HOME?
YOU'LL NEVER BE ABLE TO KEEP HIM HERE.
HE'S MY PROTECTOR.

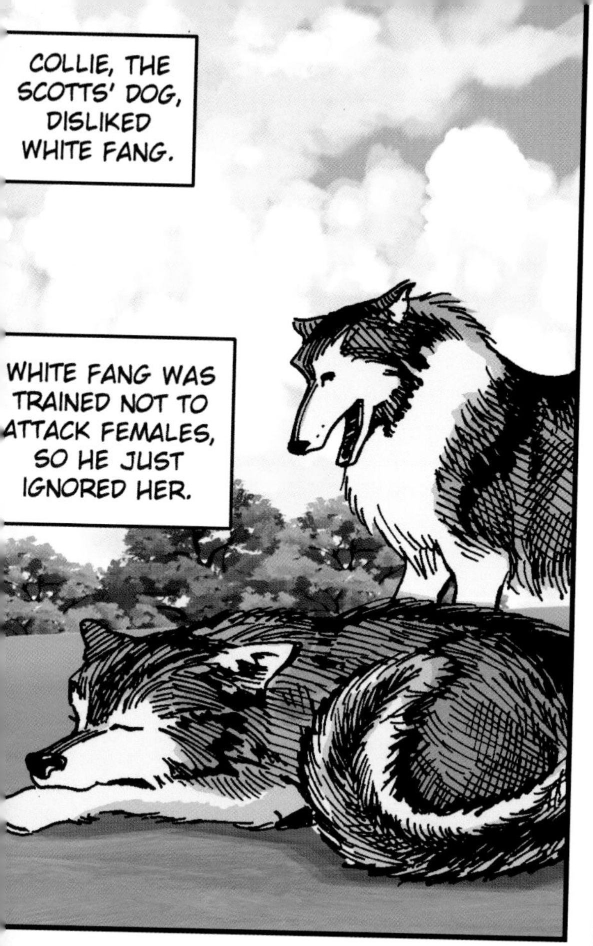
COLLIE, THE SCOTTS' DOG, DISLIKED WHITE FANG.
WHITE FANG WAS TRAINED NOT TO ATTACK FEMALES, SO HE JUST IGNORED HER.

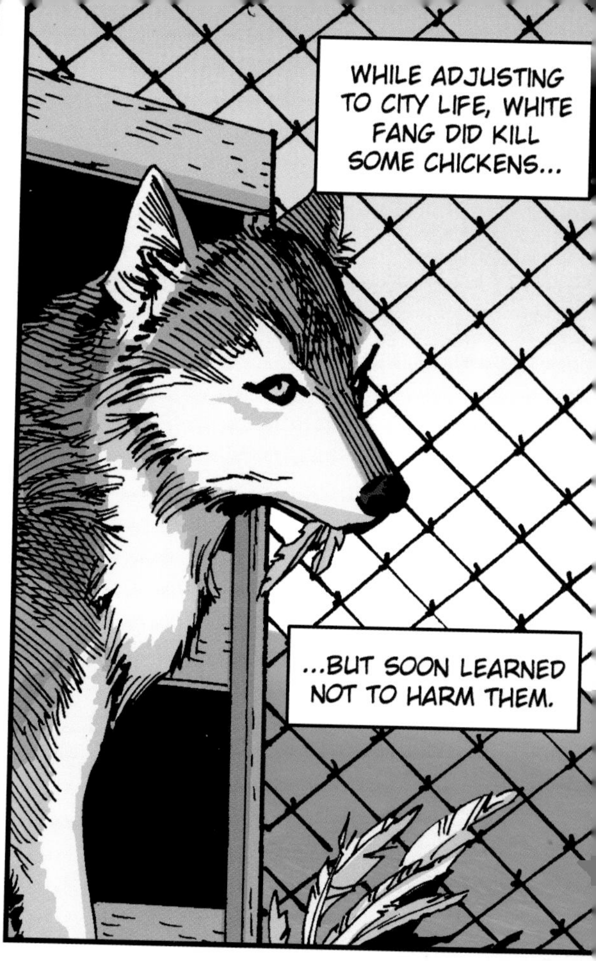
WHILE ADJUSTING TO CITY LIFE, WHITE FANG DID KILL SOME CHICKENS...
...BUT SOON LEARNED NOT TO HARM THEM.

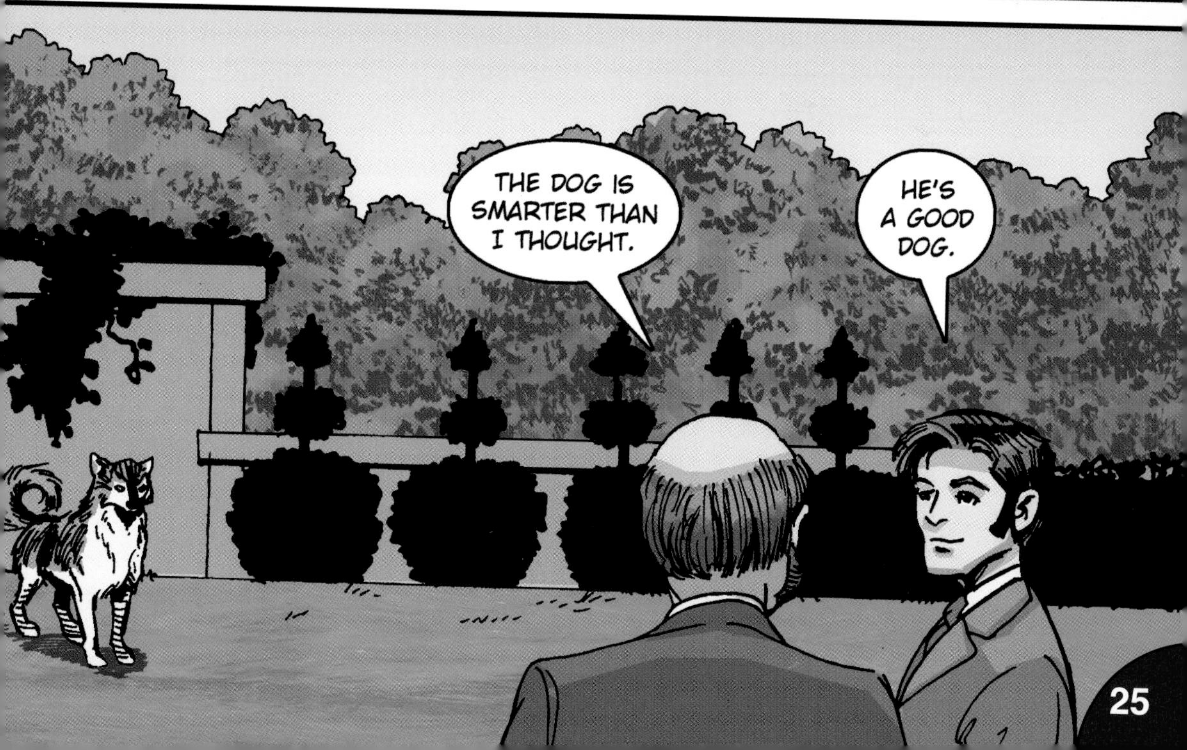
THE DOG IS SMARTER THAN I THOUGHT.
HE'S A GOOD DOG.

Chapter 6 White Fang the Hero

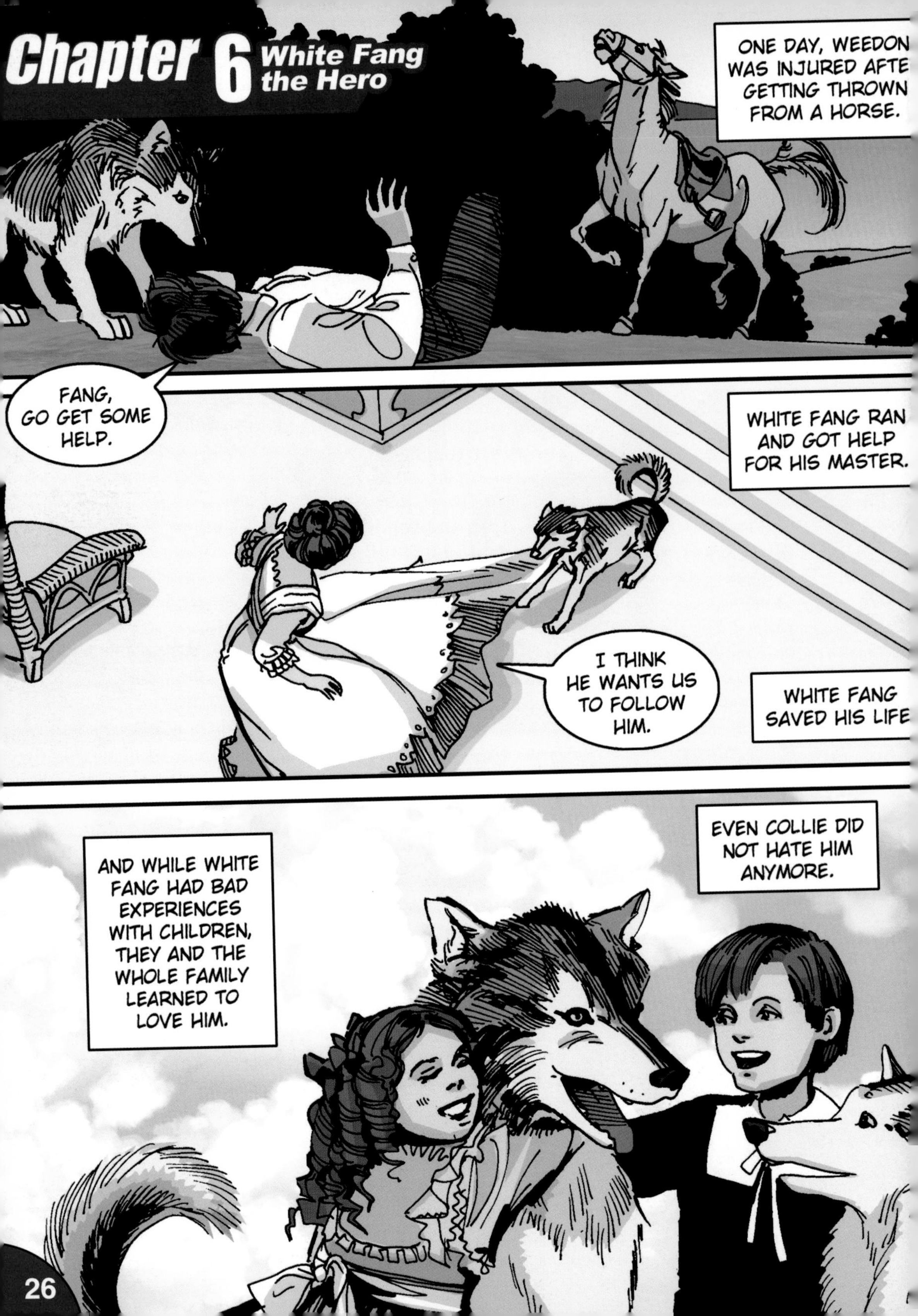
ONE DAY, WEEDON WAS INJURED AFTE GETTING THROWN FROM A HORSE.
FANG, GO GET SOME HELP.
WHITE FANG RAN AND GOT HELP FOR HIS MASTER.
I THINK HE WANTS US TO FOLLOW HIM.
WHITE FANG SAVED HIS LIFE
AND WHILE WHITE FANG HAD BAD EXPERIENCES WITH CHILDREN, THEY AND THE WHOLE FAMILY LEARNED TO LOVE HIM.
EVEN COLLIE DID NOT HATE HIM ANYMORE.

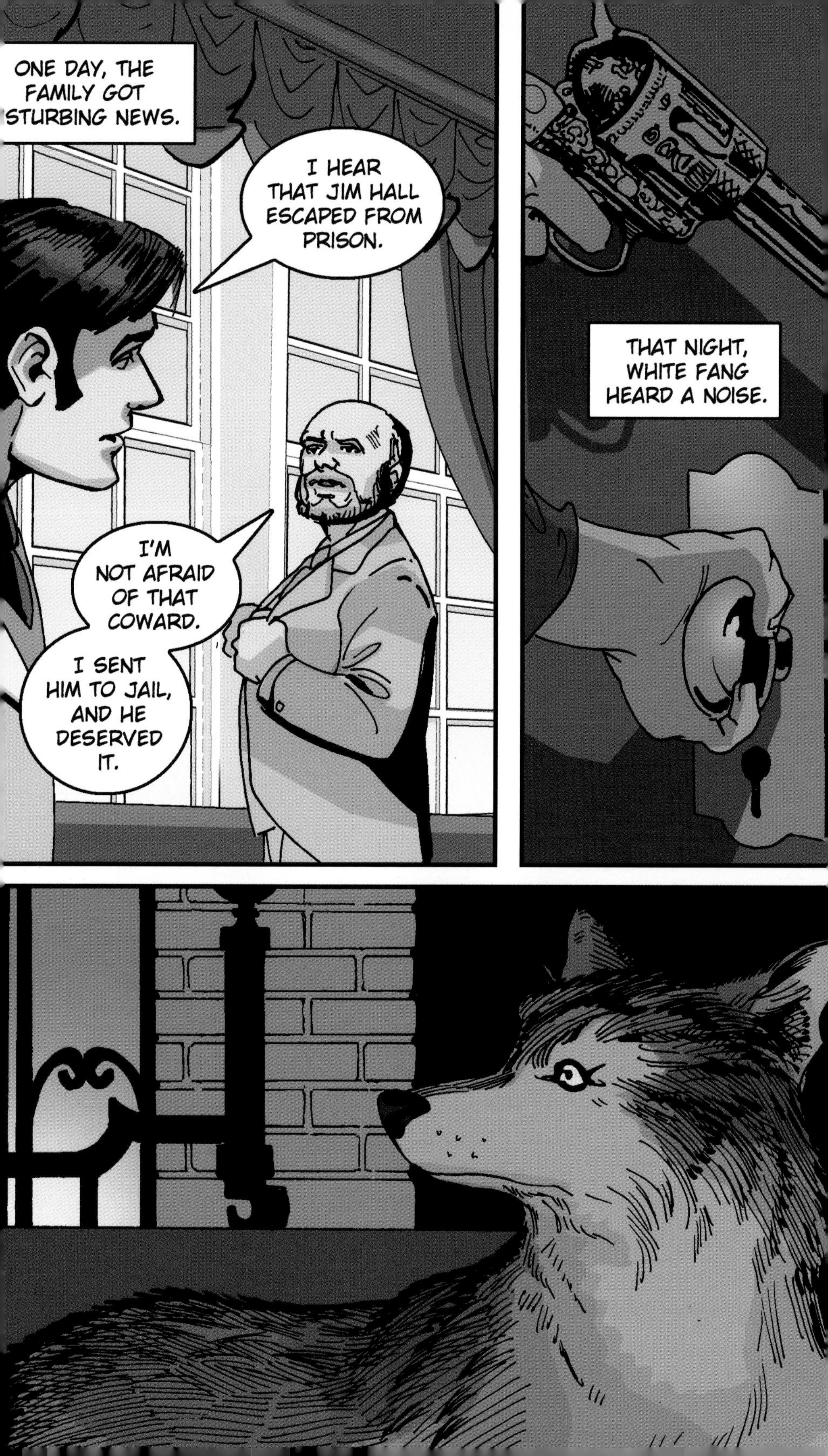
ONE DAY, THE FAMILY GOT STURBING NEWS.
I HEAR THAT JIM HALL ESCAPED FROM PRISON.
I'M NOT AFRAID OF THAT COWARD.
I SENT HIM TO JAIL, AND HE DESERVED IT.
THAT NIGHT, WHITE FANG HEARD A NOISE.

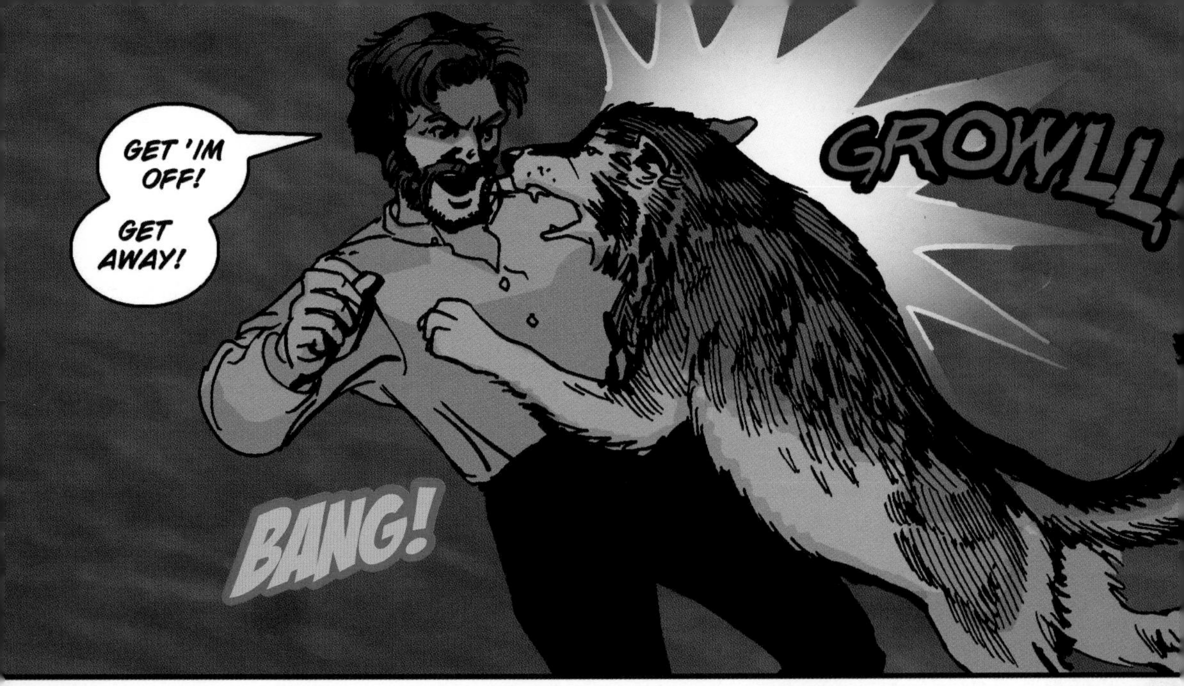
GET 'IM OFF!
GET AWAY!
GROWLL
BANG!

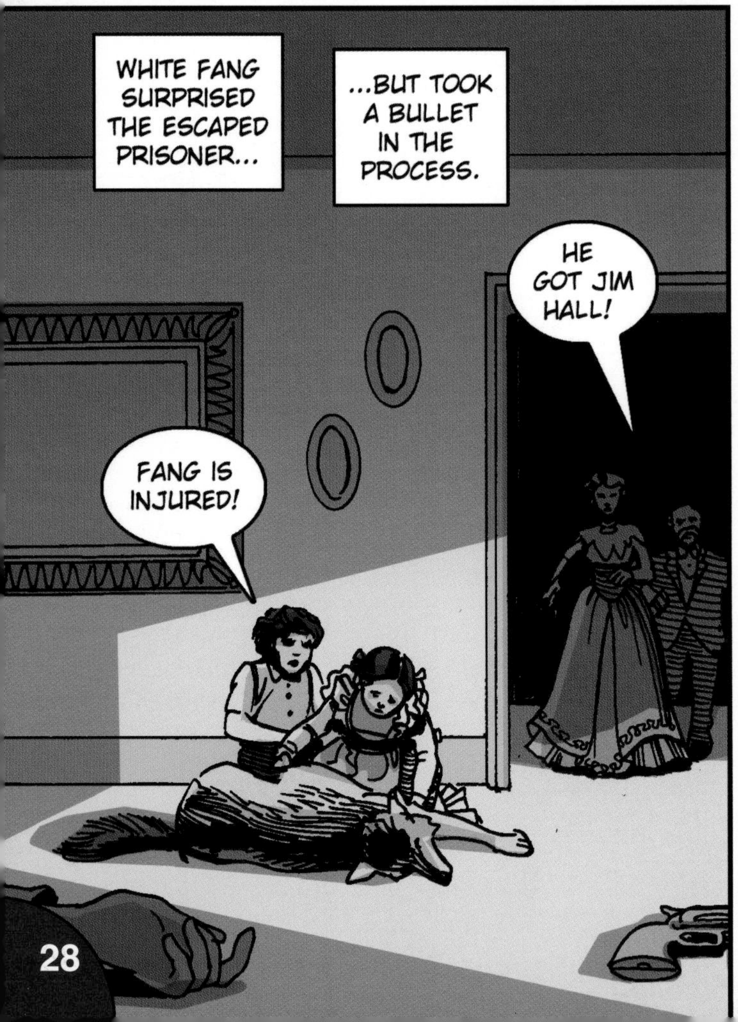
WHITE FANG SURPRISED THE ESCAPED PRISONER...
...BUT TOOK A BULLET IN THE PROCESS.
HE GOT JIM HALL!
FANG IS INJURED!

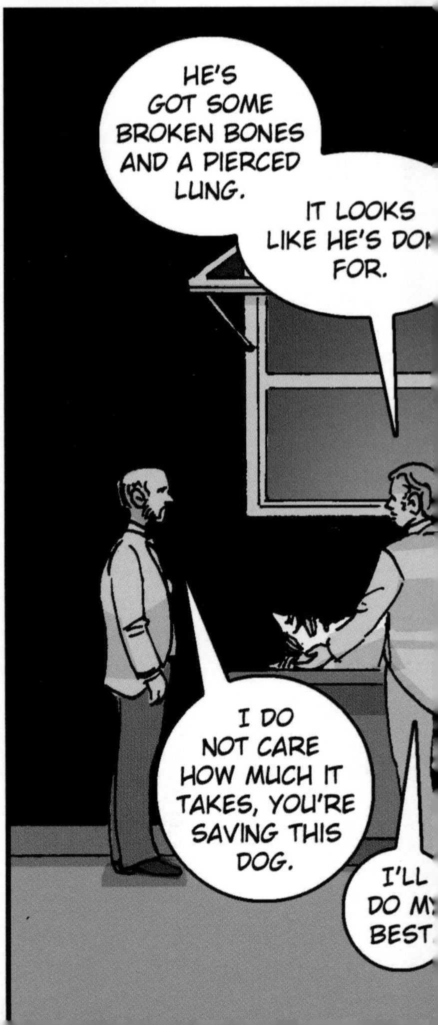
HE'S GOT SOME BROKEN BONES AND A PIERCED LUNG.
IT LOOKS LIKE HE'S DO FOR.
I DO NOT CARE HOW MUCH IT TAKES, YOU'RE SAVING THIS DOG.
I'LL DO M BEST

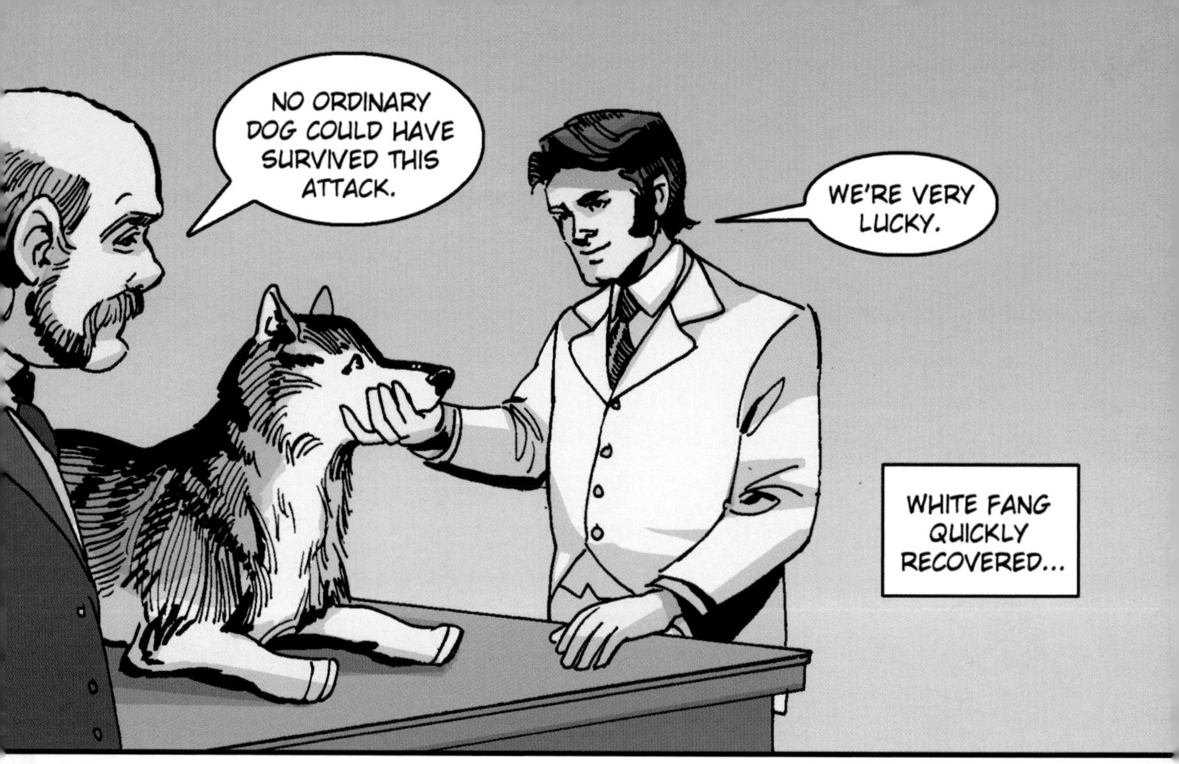
NO ORDINARY DOG COULD HAVE SURVIVED THIS ATTACK.
WE'RE VERY LUCKY.
WHITE FANG QUICKLY RECOVERED...

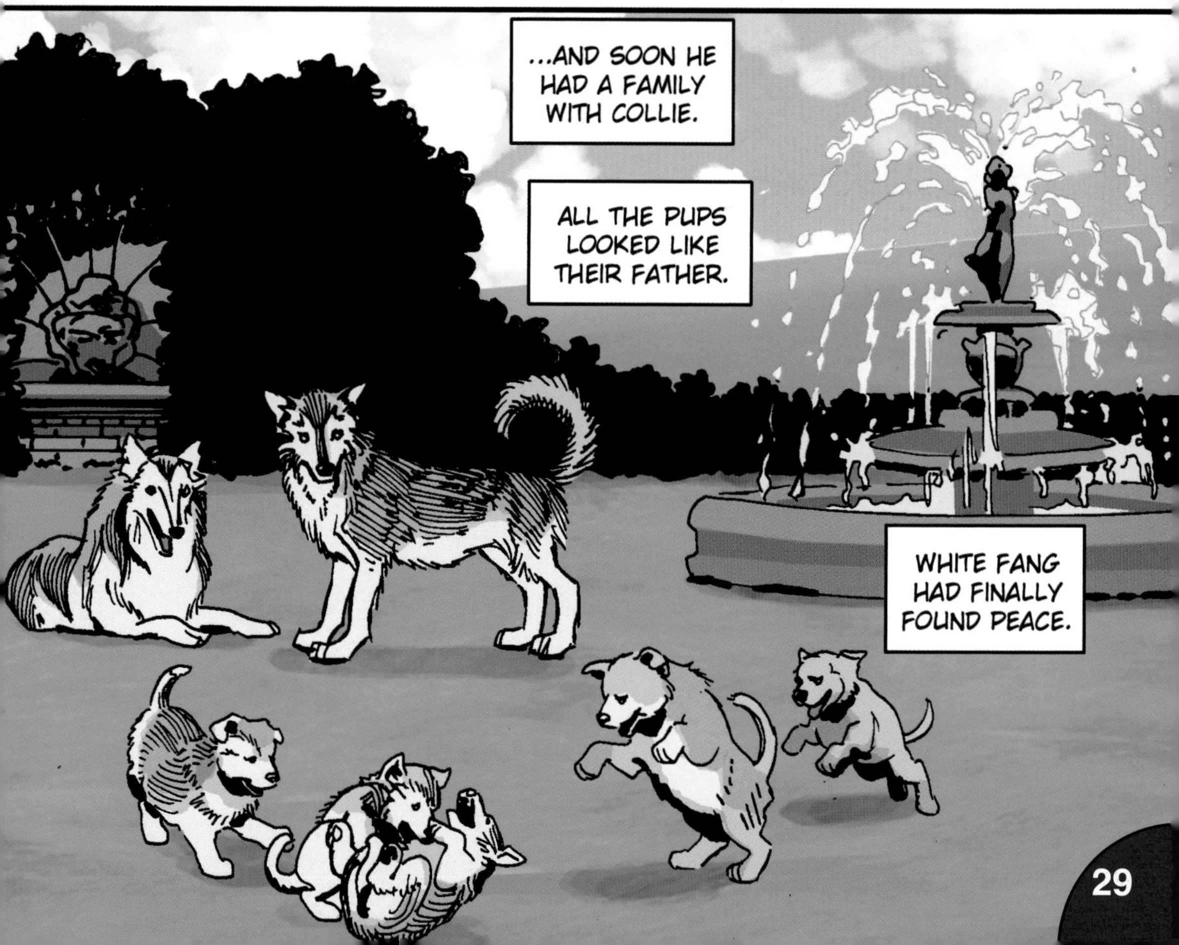
...AND SOON HE HAD A FAMILY WITH COLLIE.
ALL THE PUPS LOOKED LIKE THEIR FATHER.
WHITE FANG HAD FINALLY FOUND PEACE.

About the Author

John Griffin Chaney was born on January 12, 1876, in San Francisco, California. His father, William Henry Chaney, left the family when John was young. His mother, Flora Wellman, later married John London, and young John took his stepfather's name.

There were 12 London children, and the family lived in poverty. Young John, known as Jack, left school at the age of 14 to earn money. Between the ages of 16 and 19, he held many jobs connected to the sea. He traveled to Japan and Canada and across the United States.

London educated himself at public libraries. At 19, he completed a high school degree and then attended the University of California at Berkeley for one year. In 1897, he left Berkeley and went to the Klondike to search for gold. He returned without finding gold and decided to earn money by becoming a writer.

Over the next 14 years, London wrote nearly 50 books. He also wrote poetry, short stories, and letters. He became the most widely read American author. On November 22, 1916, London died in California. His work lives on in the many translations around the world

Additional Works

Additional Works by Jack London

The Son of the Wolf (1900)
The God of His Fathers (1901)
Children of the Frost (1902)
A Daughter of the Snows (1902)
The Call of the Wild (1903)
The Sea Wolf (1904)
The Iron Heel (1907)
Martin Eden (1909)
The Cruise of the Snark (1911)
South Sea Tales (1911)
John Barleycorn (1913)

About the Adapter

Joeming Dunn is both a general practice physician and the owner of one of the largest comic companies in Texas, Antarctic Press. A graduate of two Texas schools, Austin College in Sherman and the University of Texas Medical Branch in Galveston, he has currently settled in San Antonio.

Dr. Dunn has written or co-authored texts in both the medical and graphic novel fields. He met his wife, Teresa, in college, and they have two bright and lovely girls, Ashley and Camerin. Ashley has even helped some with his research for these Magic Wagon books.

Glossary

commotion - a noisy uproar that draws attention.

intruder - a person who enters an area, such as anothe person's home, without permission.

prospector - a person who searches for minerals, especially gold.

veteran - someone with a lot of experience.

Web Sites

To learn more about Jack London, visit ABDO Publishing Company on the World Wide Web at **www.abdopublishing.com.** Web sites abou London are featured on our Book Links page. These links are routinel monitored and updated to provide the most current information availa